First edition
Editing by Heather Osborne
Formatting by Dawn Nelson
Cover design by Terry Wells Brown

For my girls, the Sisters of Sin authors, who are so generous
with their advice, time and friendship x

Envy

D A NELSON

Chapter 1 - The Funeral

What do you mean she's dead?" Creeping cold brushed the back of Envy's neck. "When? How?" Isabella 'Izzy' Starr, code name Envy, stood with her cell to her ear, utterly devastated. Wrath had called to tell her Mother was dead, and it was Dominika who had done it.

"But why?" She could barely get the words out.

"Mother found out about Dominika's plans to take down Conexus," Wrath said. "And it was her who set the bomb."

"No!"

Izzy couldn't believe what she was hearing. It was unfathomable that one of their own had attacked their HQ, let alone had murdered their beloved leader. Elizabeth Danvers, Mother, might have been the one who assigned Izzy and her fellow assassins, the Sisters of Sin, with their jobs, but she had also been like a real mother to all of them. Including Izzy. And Dominika, for that matter.

Izzy sat down on the sofa and listened whilst Wrath took her through the funeral plans. Mother had no next of kin so they were giving her an honorary burial in the Sisters of Sin catacombs under Rome's busy streets.

"So, get here as fast as you can," Wrath concluded. "Any problems, let me know."

"I will, thanks." Izzy's head was reeling and she felt sick to her stomach. How could the girls go on without their Mother? Then a thought occurred to her. "What about Dominika? Is someone going after her? Do you want me to help?"

"Hang fire, sis," Wrath said. "I've got that in hand. She'll not get away with this."

The call disconnected, and Izzy sat back against her sofa, trying to take it all in. Then she took up her cell phone again and opened it up. Time to book a flight to Rome.

****

Izzy, dressed in a Chanel black trouser suit and white shirt, disembarked flight GLA2365 Glasgow to Rome the following afternoon, and stepped down on to the runway at Fiumicino Airport. It had been some years since she had been here, the last time was at Mother's behest to start her training as a Sister. That now seemed like a lifetime ago, and she couldn't believe she was coming here for Mother's funeral. She quickly brushed a stray tear away and followed the rest of the passengers into the Arrivals lounge. Getting through Customs was quick, and within half an hour, Izzy, trailing a Louis Vuitton carry on case, walked out of the airport and paused just outside the exit to compose herself.

A spot of rain hit her nose and she looked up at the overcast sky. The clouds were dark and grey. It was going to pour. Damnit! She hurried along looking at the cars parked in the loading bay for signs of her ride.

Finn was standing next to a black, bullet-proof limousine in the pick-up area. He saw her, waved and then rushed over and gave her a hug and kiss as a welcome.

"So lovely to see you, Envy," he said, ushering her towards the car. "I just wish it was in better circumstances." He took her carry-on case from her and handed it to the driver.

"What actually happened?" Izzy asked. "Wrath gave me a brief account; she said Dominika did it."

"Let's get into the car, and I'll tell you all about it."

During their drive to the Conexus building, the headquarters of the Sisters of Sin, Finn related what he knew. He couldn't tell her much more than she had already gleaned from Wrath. Mother had confronted Dominika about the bombing and everything she had been up to. The tall Russian assassin had retaliated by stabbing her in the heart with a knife. Despite the best efforts of the on-site health staff, they couldn't save Mother. She had been killed instantly.

"It's devastating to think that one of our own was responsible for all this," he said.

Finn's face was drawn and tired, his eyes red. He had an air of utter devastation about him, and it was no wonder. He had loved Mother for years. Everyone had known it, including Mother herself. Izzy wondered why he had never acted upon it. She leaned over and gave his hand a squeeze.

The rain was now coming down in sheets, and she was glad for the dry comfort of the luxury limousine.

****

Half an hour later, the car turned into Via della Conciliazion, where the Conexus building stood. She peered out of the window to get a better look and gasped when she saw it. The once beautiful old headquarters was now covered in scaffold, its debris netting stretching from floor to roof, coloured red and flapping wildly in the heavy downpour.

Finn leaned over and looked out too. "Don't worry," he said. "We'll soon have it up-and-running again. We managed to get the underground rooms back pretty quickly, so it's just the upper layers that need fixing."

"Was this caused by the bomb?" she asked. He nodded. "The bomb Dominika set?"

Izzy thought of her former sister and grimaced. She had never liked the disagreeable Russian, but never in her wildest dreams did she think she was capable of this. One of their own had murdered Mother and bombed the HQ. She bristled. Well, Dominika Gagolin had better watch out, she vowed. If I ever cross paths with you, you will be dead.

"Don't worry, Envy," Finn said, seeming to read her thoughts. "We've a plan to avenge Mother's death. Once the funeral is over tomorrow, Wrath is going to track her down."

Izzy angled her body toward him, inhaling deeply. "I'll help."

"No, we need you to keep working," he said. "Dominika has tried to undermine the organisation, to bring it down, but we can't let that happen. We need all you girls to continue taking jobs, to bring in the money and help us rebuild. That's the best thing you can do for us right now."

"But Dominika is powerful. She's sneaky. She'll expect us to come after her," she pointed out.

"We know," he said, "but we've got our secret weapon... Wrath."

"Okay," Izzy conceded. Despite her small size, Wrath was a powerhouse and one of the best assassins they had. "But if she needs back up, I'm there."

"She knows that."

The car entered the underground garage of the Conexus

plot and dropped Finn and Izzy off at a secure entranceway. Finn placed his hand on the biometric pad and the door slid open. With a sweep of one hand, he motioned for Izzy to enter first and followed her. They were in a small corridor that led into the main Conexus HQ underground lair. Featuring office space, staff accommodation, a gun range and armoury, labs, small hospital and a five star restaurant, the subterranean part of the complex stretched a good couple of miles. Izzy, who had, like all the other Sisters of Sin, been trained there, had never seen the entire facility, but was familiar with most of it.

"I've got you a room in the staff accommodation next door to Greed and Lust," he said, nodding to some security personnel who walked past them. "I'll get the driver to put your case in your room. For now, can I suggest we join the others in the common room for some refreshments?"

Izzy nodded, needing something to pep her up. A cup of tea and a pastry would just hit the spot, she thought, as she made her way towards one of her favourite employee areas.

****

The rest of the Sisters were already seated, enjoying some hot drinks and Italian pastries when Finn and Izzy arrived. They greeted their fellow assassin with shouts of welcome, and Greed made a space for her on the sofa next to her. While Izzy took her seat, Finn nodded to a barista stationed at a bar area in one corner. He held up two fingers and mouthed: two teas, please. The barista inclined her head and got to work, and Finn returned his attention to the girls. Present, apart from Izzy (Envy), were Wrath, Jealousy, Pride, Vanity, Lust and Passion. The sisters were not normally allowed to be altogether in one place, but this was a special occasion. The only one missing: Aggravate aka Dominika Gagolin.

"Ladies," Finn began, "it is with great sorrow that I welcome you all back today. As you know, our dear Elizabeth, the woman you all called Mother, was brutally taken from us. Plans are afoot to avenge her death, but for now I ask that we gather tomorrow at the Conexus necropolis to say our goodbyes to our dear one. As you know, it is customary for each of you to place an item in the coffin of the departed to give them a proper send-off. Many years ago, our assassins would place weapons and other items to help the dead go into the afterlife. I don't propose we do that now, but maybe a letter of farewell may be nice."

"That's an excellent idea," Greed, Alex Grier, agreed.

Finn smiled. "I'm so glad because I've arranged for you all to have Smythson of Bond Street writing paper and Graf von Faber-Castell pens in your rooms. Only the very best for Mother."

The barista appeared holding two large tea cups and saucers of steaming tea. Finn took them and handed one to Izzy. Finn then raised his cup.

"I know that this is only tea—one of Mother's favourite drinks—and we will have something stronger for her wake tomorrow, but can we raise our cups and drink to her?" He waited until cups and mugs were raised. "To Mother."

"To Mother," the assassins chorused.

****

Mother was being laid to rest early the next morning, and Izzy woke at six to ensure she was ready on time. After a quick shower, she put up her dark hair into a chignon and slipped into a black sheath dress. Sliding her feet into court shoes, she picked up a white envelope containing her letter to Mother and placed a knife in a sheath around one thigh… just in case. Then she had a simple breakfast of pastries and coffee with Greed in the Conexus restaurant.

At 7.40am, she and Greed then joined the rest of the Sisters and Conexus staff on the slow procession to the Conexus Church of All Faiths situated on a level below. The column of mourners walked to the end of the complex and through two large steel doors. They were now leaving modern underground facility and, Izzy mused, walking back in time.

A downwards sloping walkway took them further into the bowels of the Earth, into the most ancient part of the Conexus campus. The smooth walls, electric lights and wide marble floors soon gave way to a slim walkway lined with ancient bricks and worn stone floor tiles. There was no electricity here, but the way was lit by a multitude of candles on wall sconces. It seemed to take forever to reach their destination, but at last they turned a corner and the corridor widened again to reveal the arched entranceway to the basilica beyond.

The Church was many hundreds of years old and had originally been for Roman Catholic worship. However, with more and more employees joining of different faiths and backgrounds, a decision had been taken some 20 years previously to change it to a church welcoming all faiths. A non-believer, Izzy rarely stepped inside any religious buildings, but she appreciated them for what they were and for their historical value. Having never been in the Conexus church before, she found it fascinating.

Built some 20 metres underground, the church was obviously very old. It had a high, vaulted ceiling and walls painted with biblical scenes. At one end was the sanctuary, where the altar was, and a gorgeously carved wooden pulpit to the right.

There were various religious artefacts from a number of different faiths arranged on a purple velvet cloth on the altar, along with a gold and bejewelled tabernacle. The church pews were arranged in rows on either side of an aisle and could seat up to 100 worshippers.

The Sisters took their seats in the front row of the pews with the remainder of the staff sitting in the rows behind. Over some free-standing speakers, The Beatles' song 'Somewhere' suddenly started up (Mother's favourite), a cue that the funeral had begun. As one, the congregation rose and turned to face the entrance-way.

Izzy stifled a sob when she saw a heart-broken Finn, in a black suit and carrying a leather folder, walk down the aisle ahead of six male mourners solemnly carrying Mother's casket. Izzy, so calm beforehand, saw the beautiful wooden coffin with the British Union flag draped over it and suddenly the whole enormity of what she was witnessing hit her. Before she could stop them, big fat tears rolled down her cheeks and she was overwhelmed by the knowledge that this was Mother and she would never see her again. She felt an arm go around her waist and turned to see that it was Greed hugging her. She leaned in and accepted the comfort. Life was never going to be the same again.

Finn climbed up into the pulpit and stood with his head bowed whilst the coffin bearers carefully placed Mother's coffin on a stand nearby. The music receded, and at Finn's behest, the congregation sat down. He cleared his throat and opened his folder, placing it on shelf in front of him.

"Ladies and gentlemen," he began. "Thank you all for coming today to celebrate the life of Elizabeth Danvers, Mother to many of you." His voice cracked. "As you know, Elizabeth's life was abruptly cut short by one of our own. But today, we are not going to dwell on her passing, but remember her as the wonderful person she was."

****

Izzy barely remembered what had happened for the rest of the service. Two more of Mother's favourite Beatles' tracks were played, and some staff members were invited down to the front to recount fond memories of her. As the service came to an end, Finn lifted a white envelope from his folder and opened it, withdrawing the letter from inside.

"Our jobs can be dangerous, and Elizabeth knew that one day her time would come, so she gave me this letter to read out to you all at her funeral."

There were gasps all round. This was something Izzy hadn't reckoned on and she was sure her Sisters felt the same.

Finn took a deep breath and began: "My dear colleagues and friends, if you are reading this I must be dead. I hope my death was a good one and not too grisly."

There were a few titters around the room. Mother had always joked she was going to die elegantly with a cocktail in her hand.

Finn continued: "Anyway, I just want to let you all know just how privileged I was to work with you. To the Conexus staff: I could not have done everything I did without your help. You have all been marvellous to work with and I wish you all beautiful and happy lives."

Here, he paused to let the words sink in. Then he looked down at the Sisters of Sin sitting in the front row. "To my beloved girls, the Sisters of Sin, you are unique in each and every way, and I love you all very much. You are all, without exception, some of the most talented and clever women I have ever had the honour to work with and I think of you all as my actual children."

Izzy let out a loud sob and Greed pulled her in for a hug.

"And finally, to my righthand man and best friend…" Finn paused, wiped a tear from his eye and composed himself. "…best friend, Finn. It has been wonderful being your friend, and I will always love you." He took a silk handkerchief from his pocket and blew his nose. "So, there you go everyone, that's me on my way to a new adventure. Goodbye, dear friends, I wish you all the very best. Love Elizabeth, your Mother."

You could have heard a pin drop; the church was so silent. Finn nodded to the coffin bearers who were seated in the second row. As one, they rose and came forward to take up their positions again under Mother's casket. They lifted it on to their shoulders and adjusted it, ready to take it to its final resting place.

"Please rise," Finn said. The congregation got to their feet. "Now, please, will the Sisters follow me as we take Mother on her final journey to her final resting place."

The pallbearers lead the way to a large wooden arched door with metal studs in the side of the church. Slowly, the solemn procession made its way into yet another brick passageway to the catacombs beyond. As they reached the doorway, each person was handed a lit candle to help them light the way.

Izzy was not claustrophobic, but even she was starting to get uneasy as the group made their way down an increasingly narrow passageway that had been cut into rock. Where were they going? And what would they see when they got there? They passed indents in the walls—shelving resembling bunks that were large enough to hold bodies. And as they walked further, the candlelight began to pick out coffins: wooden, metal, leather-covered with gold studs, each reflecting the time in history they had been put there.

"Former assassins," Finn explained when he saw her looking at them in awe. "They are given the honour of being buried here in the Conexus catacombs."

"Right," she replied, "and will Mother…?"

He put his finger to his lips. "All will be revealed," he said.

The procession walked on before coming to a halt outside another heavy wooden door with huge black studs. Finn removed a large iron key from his jacket pocket, slipped it into the door's old lock and turned it. The key turned easily and allowed him to throw open the door. Holding his candle aloft, he walked into the burial chamber closely followed by the pall bearers and the Sisters.

Mother's coffin was placed on a marble plinth, and the bearers, heads bowed, backed out of the vault leaving Finn with the seven assassins. They gathered around the coffin, candles in hand, and stood in silence for a moment. Then Finn sighed and stepped forward. He carefully opened the top half of the coffin lid to reveal a serene Mother, in a simple silk dress, lying peacefully on a silken pillow. Her hands were folded on her stomach.

She looked beautiful, Izzy thought. The funeral directors had done such a good job with the body, it was almost as if she was just sleeping.

Finn turned to the girls. "So, this is the time where we say our traditional goodbye to Mother," he said. "Can you, one by one, bring forward your gift for Mother and lay it in the coffin at her side?"

He focused on Izzy. "Envy, can you go first?"

Fighting back the tears, Izzy stepped forward, her pristine

white envelope containing her letter to Mother in trembling hands. Slipping her envelope into the coffin, she whispered, "Goodbye, Mother."

As soon as she was done, the next Sister stepped forward and did the same, followed by another. A few minutes later, all the girls had said their goodbyes, and it was left to Finn to finish the farewell. He pulled his own envelope from his breast pocket, kissed it and placed it under Mother's cold hands. Then he lowered the coffin lid and stepped back.

"Farewell, darling Elizabeth," he said. "You will be in our heart, always."

****

Finn had arranged for the Conexus chef, Nero Caballi, to lay on an expansive buffet for the mourners in the staff restaurant. Beautifully cooked traditional Italian dishes— ranging from seafood and pasta, and pizzas and salads, to pastries and cakes—weighed down several large tables. At a separate table was the bar, and it was to here that Izzy beelined. It had been a stressful couple of days, and she felt in need of something cold and bubbly.

Champagne flutes filled to the brim with the best French Champagne was laid out in six short rows and she grabbed a glass. Taking a sip, she sighed with relief as the chilled liquid slid down her parched throat. She had sobbed at the service, cried in the crypt and had sniffled all the way back to the upper level. She wasn't normally so publicly emotional, but Mother had been special, and she was going to miss her. The sting of tears pricked her eyes again.

"Oh, for God's sake, will you quit it?" It was Wrath. The diminutive assassin stood, hands on hips, and glared at Izzy.

Izzy wiped her eyes with her free hand and sniffed. "Sorry."

"I know it's sad Mother has gone, but she wouldn't want you to ruin that pretty face of yours, would she?" Wrath asked. She put her arm around Izzy's waist and gave her a squeeze.

"I suppose not," Izzy replied.

"Good. Now get some more of that down you," she said, pointing at Izzy's glass of Champagne, "while I go and attack the buffet table. I'm starving."

****

The following day as Izzy was saying goodbye to her fellow Sisters, Wrath took her aside.

"I've got a job for you," she said, pushing a memory stick into Izzy's hands. "It's right up your street…a businessman who is responsible for the murders of indigenous people in the Amazon basin."

"But don't you want me to help you track down Dominika?" Since learning of Mother's death, all Izzy had wanted was to sink a knife in Dominika's black heart.

"No, babe, I got it," Wrath replied. Izzy began to protest, but was cut off. "Look, I need you girls to keep working so that the business continues. Jeff Lynsey is…"

"Jeff Lynsey? I thought he was dead!"

"He's alive along with a couple of the other board members. Anyway, Jeff is empire-building at the moment, so as well as killing Dominika, I've got that to deal with. So, if you girls could just keep going, that would be awesome."

Izzy looked at Wrath and for the first time saw the pain in her Sister's eyes. Wrath was normally so in control and unflappable, but Izzy could see Mother's murder had got to her. She gave her a hug.

"No problem."

"Thanks, sister!"

****

In a private safe house some distance from Rome, Dominika Gagolin plotted her next move. She wasn't finished with the Sisters of Sin or Conexus yet, not in any way. Now Mother was dead—she smiled as she remembered plunging the hot knife into Mother's chest—the organisation was ripe for being crushed under her six-inch Jimmy Choos.

Dominika sat back in her leather office chair and smiled. Yes, before long, she would be the Queen Bee in the assassination world, and she wouldn't be quite so picky about the jobs. Her team wouldn't just take out the nasties of the world. Her team would do any job she told them to. Yes, it will be fun taking out world leaders and watching the world's superpowers come crashing down!

Chapter 2 - Fleming

The Georgian townhouse in London's fashionable Grosvenor Square was dark and quiet. The staff had gone for the night, the householders were elsewhere and the only living things were the tropical fish that swam around and around in a massive illuminated tank in the living room. That was, except for the one human waiting patiently, quietly, on the living room sofa for the master of the house to return.

Izzy sat and contemplated the job ahead. She was here to eliminate a businessman with a very shady past who had murdered scores of innocent people. For that alone she was tempted to take her time in killing him, maybe even torture him a little, but his trophy wife, the bimbo she had seen leave the house an hour earlier, could come home at any time. Better wait for him, do the deed and leave as quickly and quietly as she had entered.

It hadn't been hard to get access to this heavily alarmed home. Izzy had a knack with electronics and had shut the alarm off within a minute. No, the longest time she had spent on this job was casing the family, learning their habits. She knew he would come home around seven and fix himself a whisky. Then she would pounce.

The only fly in the ointment to her plan was the man's long-haired, fake-boobed other half. Yes, the little wifey was a possible issue. Izzy had no idea where she had gone or when she was due back, but her target's better half had been dressed to the nines when she had left, so Izzy was taking an educated guess that the she was out for the night. That would give her more than enough time.

Izzy stroked the handgun nestled on her lap. It was her favourite piece, a Beretta 92 service pistol that had been gifted to her by an ex-US army captain as a thank you for a small job she had done for him once. It was a vintage piece, but dependable and she had used it many times on jobs. Speaking of which…

Now, where was the man of the moment?

Industrialist Bob Fleming was a boorish, arrogant man who was not above stepping outside the law to further his business interests. Fraudulent practises, bribery of officials and stealing were all on his conscience, as was the systematic murder of indigenous South American tribespeople who dared to stand up to him and his company's interests there. According to the file Wrath had given her on the memory stick, to-date, more than thirty tribal protesters had been despatched by Fleming's goons, but God knows how many more bodies were hidden in the Amazon rainforest. He was a ruthless, slippery man who stopped at nothing to turn a profit. So far, the international police had failed to get him on any charge, so it was up to Izzy, hired by persons unknown, to rid the world of the 57-year-old menace once and for all.

And she would enjoy it.

Izzy ran her gloved hand over the dark nubuck sofa and inhaled its sweet leathery smell. An expensive designer sofa in an expensively furnished home, a house neither she nor all her ancestors put together could ever have afforded. Although, in saying that, she wouldn't thank you for living here, in the smog of

London. She was a country girl at heart. Her tall slim body sank into the fine upholstery giving her the overwhelming feeling of relaxation and wellbeing. In other circumstances, she could have just sat back and enjoyed the sensation, but she wasn't here to relax. She was here to spill blood. Although she would regret spilling it all over Fleming's Chinese silk rug.

How many people did you fuck over to afford that?

Izzy was happy to kill Fleming. Had she not needed the money, she might even have done it for free. Izzy hated bullies, she hated the companies who stripped the land of its goodness, and she hated businesses that knowingly worked to bring the Earth one step closer to midnight on the Doomsday Clock. She was a woman of conscience when it came to the environment and to the innocents who had been murdered in trying to protect it. Bob Fleming and his cronies were causing untold long-term damage to the world, and they needed to be stopped. Cut off the head and the snake died. Take out Bob and his international business interests would be thrown into disarray long enough for things to turn around.

She hoped.

No matter, Izzy would still enjoy killing him, if nothing else than to avenge those men and women who had died defending their lands.

In the darkness, she smiled. He was getting what was coming to him.

Outside, a car drew up, and a door banged closed. Footsteps clipped up the external stone stairs leading to Fleming's front door and a keypad beeped. The door opened, and the hall light was switched on.

Izzy heard him throw keys on the hallway table and then the distinctive steps of his hand-made Italian shoes on the marble floor. He was heading towards the living room for his habitual evening drink.

Having left the door ajar, she watched him from her shadowy position on the sofa as he made his way toward the bar at the rear of the room. He switched on a lamp, its glow illuminating that corner of the room, and fetched a crystal glass from beneath the bar. He carefully placed it on the bar-top and opened a crystal whisky decanter.

He was a tall man, balding, with sagging cheek jowls and a physique that was more beer barrel than six pack. He will be easy to take down, Izzy thought, as she watched him swig from the glass.

"Aren't you going to pour me one?" Izzy asked, her Scottish accent soft and singsong.

Fleming jumped, nearly dropping his glass. Izzy leant over and switched on a lamp on a table next to her. It illuminated her lithe body and beautiful face.

"Hello, Mr Fleming," she said with a smile.

"Who are you? What are you doing in my house?"

Izzy pulled her gun from her lap and held it up for him to see. "To put it bluntly," she said, giving him her sweetest smile, "I'm here to kill you."

Fleming froze, and Izzy could see from the horrified expression on his craggy face that he was trying hard to think of a way out. He opened his mouth and took a deep breath to shout, but immediately exhaled when she trained the gun on him.

"I wouldn't do that, if I were you," she said smoothly. "In fact, never mind me. Go ahead! No-one's going to hear you anyway. Your wife is out, the staff are gone for the day and these lovely old houses are so well built, your neighbours won't hear a peep. So, go ahead. Scream as loud as you want. It will only make the killing more pleasurable."

She could see he was considering it, his face a myriad of expressions. Then he looked at her with frightened eyes and bit his lip. She could see he was trying to pull himself together enough to ask a question.

"What do you want?" His voice was weak, croaky.

"You've annoyed some very important people, Mr Fleming" she said, tutting. "And I'm afraid they don't want you to continue living."

With trembling fingers, he poured himself another whisky and took a gulp. "Might I ask who?"

"You can ask, but I can't tell you," she said.

The truth was she didn't know. Izzy was usually handed her jobs by Mother at the Sisters of Sin HQ in Italy. All she knew was who the target was and a bit of background. Who had ordered the hit was none of her business. Oh, Mother! She felt grief rise its ugly head again. She still couldn't believe she was gone.

There was a pause whilst he took another drink. "I suppose they are paying you handsomely for this?"

"Good enough," she replied, getting to her feet. She sauntered towards him, gun in hand.

"Well, how about I double that…no, treble it?" he asked. There was hope in his voice, in his eyes. "I'm a very wealthy man, you know, and I'll pay you whatever you want. Whatever they're offering you, I will triple it."

He actually thinks he can buy me off, she thought. Fool.

Izzy smiled. "Attractive proposition," she said, "but I can't possibly accept. You see, I don't like bullies, and you've been a bit of a bully in your business life, haven't you, Mr Fleming? In fact, the bullying has been so bad, you've even resorted to murdering innocents. We can't have that, now, can we?"

She raised the gun and took aim. The blood rushed from Fleming's face and he looked like he was about to be sick. A trickle of sweat ran down his forehead.

"Are you feeling okay, Mr Fleming? You look a little warm," she said.

"I…please don't kill me, I'll do anything you want." He put his glass down.

"Is that what the tribespeople said when your men murdered them in cold blood?" She took the safety off.

"What tribespeople? I don't know what you're talking about." His voice was getting increasingly desperate.

"Uh-huh, no lying, please. We both know you know all about it, don't you, Mr Fleming? At the last count, there were thirty dead, but there could be more," she said, watching him closely.

She saw him flinch when she said the word 'more'. Shit, he'd had more than thirty people murdered. Bastard.

"One of the reasons why you're getting taken out tonight is to avenge the deaths of seven of those Amazonian tribespeople. They were getting a bit too vocal for your liking. People were starting to listen to what they were saying about how your company was stripping the land of all its goodness and destroying miles of forests. So, you had them killed."

"I did not do such a thing, of course I didn't." He loosened his tie and undid the top button of his shirt. Sweat poured down his face. "Look, why don't we come to some sort of arrangement? I'll do anything, I'll even pay their families compensation or something."

"Sorry, but a contract is a contract."

Before she could stop him, he leaned over the bar and pulled a handgun of his own from behind it. Smiling, he pointed it at her. "Well, we seem to have come to a bit of an impasse, haven't we?" he said. "How quickly do you think you can squeeze that trigger?"

Izzy looked at him coolly. "I'm a fairly good shot."

"Well, I'm much better," he snarled and pulled the trigger. Nothing happened. He gaped at his gun in horror.

"Looking for these?" Izzy asked, opening her left hand and showing him a round of cartridges. "I took the trouble of checking this room for weapons. Oopsy."

He looked like he was going to pass out and tears sprang to his eyes. "Please! You can't kill me," he said eyes wide and desperate. "That would be murder. Besides, I have a family. They need me."

"Yes, you're right, it would be, but that's never stopped you, has it, Mr Fleming?" she asked. "And as for your family…well, I'm sure they'll do okay without you. A murderer."

"I've never murdered anyone in my life."

"Not personally, but you ordered your men to do it, didn't you?" She looked at her watch. "Well, I'd like to say it's been a pleasure meeting you, but that would be a lie. In precisely one minute, you'll be dead and I'll be collecting my pay."

"What? How?" His speech was slurring.

"Well, that's exactly how long it takes for the poison to work. Are your lips tingling? It usually starts in the lips."

"What?"

"I poisoned your glass before you came in. I wanted to use Curare from South America, it seemed like the obvious choice, but I couldn't get any in time. Instead, I've used an old favourite: strychnine. It should be working by now. You can expect convulsions and a slow-ish death from asphyxia. I'd love to keep you company while you die, but I have other things to do." She sheathed her gun in a holster hidden underneath her jacket and watched as he slowly began to drop, his shaking hands desperately trying to clutch the bar-top.

"Please…" Fleming gasped before sliding behind the bar and dropping to the ground.

Izzy leant over the bar smiling as the older man twitched and shook, foaming at the mouth, his eyes wild in terror. This bastard deserved everything he got.

"Well, at least now you can't ruin people's lives…but, wait a minute, your company is still operating. I wonder what would happen if someone broke into your home office and accessed all its files? Then that someone released those files to all news agencies!"

The sounds of gargling could be heard from the bar area.

"Yes, I agree, that's exactly what I'm going to do. We can't leave it to go on destroying people's lives, now can we?" She took a memory stick from her pocket and waved it so that he could see it. "Now, where do I find your office?" She stared at him. "First floor? Higher up?" He flinched. "I thought so." He mumbled something. "What's that? I couldn't make that out." She turned and began walking towards the living room door. "Goodbye Mr Fleming."

Izzy stood at the bottom of the marble staircase and thought for a moment. Now where would a bastard like Fleming keep his computer? Earlier, she had searched the sumptuous rooms of the ground floor and the high-tech kitchen in the basement, but no office was to be found. So, that only left the upstairs. She took out her gun and ascended the staircase slowly, her gloved hand on the smooth cold marble bannister for support. As she climbed, she walked past numerous oil paintings and other artworks from contemporary artists many of whom she had never heard of.

On the first-floor landing, Izzy paused and inspected at an enormous oil painting of Fleming and his family. He stood, an arrogant smirk on his face, as his wife leant into him, smiling. At their feet, sat his three children from his first marriage. None of them smiled. Despite the fact she knew him to be a rogue, Izzy couldn't help but be affected by the family group. She had never known what it was like to have been part of a family, growing up with her brother in care. Her mother, a junkie and alcoholic, had had a brief fling with a musician from Motherwell. He'd already left when she'd discovered she was pregnant with Izzy. They'd reconciled long enough to also have Izzy's younger brother, Frank, and then he'd fucked off again.

Her mother, who had kicked drugs and drink to be 'a better mother to my kids', spiralled out of control. She swan-dived into addiction again and the kids were put into care. Izzy had been three, her brother one. Neither of them remembered their parents. All they had known was being in care and foster home, after foster home, after foster home. It wasn't that Izzy and her brother were a handful. It was that the older they got, the more difficult it was to find a home for a sullen teen and her angry brother.

Izzy thought about Frank and her broken heart ached. Not a cliched 'oh, that always happens' kind of way but a literal pain. A deep pain that sat in the middle of her chest and never went away. You see, her heart had split almost completely into two the day she found out he had been murdered, and only held together from the thinnest thread of membrane. It had taken three full years before she had begun to feel alive again, but she never forgot him.

Izzy inhaled deeply. Pull it together, girl. Don't let this get to you. Taking another deep breath, she moved away from the painting and began to open doors in the long hallway.

One thing Izzy liked about rich people's houses was the fact they always had deep carpeting, which not only muffled her footsteps, but sprung back immediately, obliterating any tell-tale signs that she had been there. As she hurried along the corridor, opening door after door, it soon became clear to her that this floor only harboured a set of perfectly matching, beautifully decorated bedrooms, a linen closet packed with fragrant towels and bedroom sets, and two large dressing rooms: one for the lady of the house and one for the master.

The last door was slimmer, smaller, less conspicuous than the others and led into a carpeted stairwell. Izzy ascended slowly. For some unknown reason, she suddenly felt afraid that she was not the only person in the house. The stairwell led up to another door that opened into an attic bedroom and, at last, to Fleming's home office.

The attic room was fully carpeted and had wall to ceiling bookcases . I never thought Fleming a reader, she thought as she took in the scene. Directly in front of her, a table lamp burned dully on a large antique wooden desk illuminating the trio of screens belonging to a state-of-the-art desktop computer.

"Bingo!" Izzy murmured and stepped towards it, holding her gun.

"Who's there?" The voice was young, weak, frightened.

Izzy spun around and realised for the first time, she was not alone.

Chapter 3 - Aaron

In a darkened corner almost obscured from view, was a large double bed. On the bed a small figure was hurriedly covering its body with the duvet. Izzy located the overhead light switch, revealing the thin figure of a boy. He was staring at her, terrified, clutching the covers to his white body as if they were about to be whipped away to reveal his nakedness. He looked young, malnourished and had unkempt hair and dark circles under his eyes.

"Who are you?" she demanded.

The boy didn't answer, but continued to stare at her, eyes wide, fear muting his response.

"I said who are you?"

The boy blanched and tried to talk, but no words would come.

She waved the gun. "Answer me!"

He whimpered. "Aaron…Aaron Brown, miss," he replied in a Scottish accent.

"What kind of a name is Aaron?"

"My mum was an Elvis fan. I'm lucky it wasn't Elvis."

"And how old are you?"

"Sixteen, miss."

She stared at him. "That's not a local accent. What are you

doing in Bob Fleming's office, all the way down here in London?"

The boy didn't seem to know how to answer.

"Cat got your tongue?" she asked. She walked towards him, and he began to whimper.

"N-n-n-no."

"Then answer me."

He took a breath. "I…work…for Mr Fleming…sometimes…"

"And what do you do for him? Or shouldn't I ask?"

"He pays me to…" With his hands, he made a rude gesture.

She looked at him shocked by his confession. "You're a bit young for that, aren't you? And why bring you here? In his home? Wasn't he worried his wife would come home and catch you?"

"Naw, she's away doing some other bloke," he said matter-of-factly. "They're a right pair, they are." Then he paused and nervously bit his lip. "Are you going to kill me?" he asked, fixated on the gun in her hand.

Izzy thought about it, but looked at this young waif with pity and wondered why such a vulnerable young boy was turning tricks. Was he being forced into it? Probably. She decided to give him a break. "No, I'm not going to kill you."

"Oh, that's a relief." He visibly relaxed. "So, what are you doing here? With a gun?"

"Never you mind," she replied. "I'll let you go this time, but you never saw me tonight. Got it?"

"Deal." Then it was as if he suddenly became aware that he was lying in bed naked. "Do you know when Mr Fleming is coming? He's paid for the night. Well, until he gets tired of me."

"Mr Fleming won't be coming ever again." Izzy smirked at the innuendo.

"What do you mean?" He looked down and then back at her. "Has something happened to him?" Then his eyes widened. "Did you kill him?"

She didn't know how to answer and decided the truth would be best. "Yes, and his wife could come home any time soon, so if you don't want to be embroiled in a murder case, I'd suggest you go home and forget you ever saw me, okay?"

"Okay."

"Now, get dressed whilst I have a quick look through Fleming's computer. I assume you have clothes with you?"

Aaron nodded.

"Good, then chop, chop. I don't have all night." Then she waggled the gun again and added: "Quickly. You really don't want me to change my mind!"

While Aaron scrambled to get dressed, Izzy walked back to the desk and returned her attention to the computer. Sitting down on a large leather office chair, she switched the computer on and the multiple screens flickered into life. In the centre screen, the computer asked for a password. Damnit!

"Any idea what his password might be?" she shouted to the boy. She looked up to see him pulling on his jeans.

"No. Sorry," he said, blushing.

"Hmph."

Izzy took out her mobile phone and scrolled through notes she'd taken about Fleming and his life: wife's name, kids' names, family pets, his yacht, his first company. She typed them all in, but came up short. The computer rejected every single one of them. Reclining back in the chair, Izzy inspected the attic space.

Apart from the desk and bed and the numerous bookcases, the room, with its supporting wooden pillars, was relatively empty, save for some black and white photos of a younger looking Bob Fleming on the walls and a small drinks cabinet nearby, on top of which sat a glass case containing a stuffed rat.

Izzy stood up and strode towards it. She looked in. The dead rat, dark brown in colour, stared back with beady black glass eyes. She shuddered. She never could understand why anyone would have a stuffed animal in their house. Then a small brass plaque on the base of the case caught her eye. It read: Mr Snuffles, 1989. I wonder, she thought, and scurried back to the desk. Izzy typed in Mr Snuffles 89. Nothing. Then Mr Snuffles 1989. Nothing. Then: Snuffles89. Ping. The computer opened, and she smiled. Taking a memory stick from her pocket, she slotted it into the computer.

"What are you doing?" Aaron, now fully dressed and wearing a lime green baseball cap, stood in front of the desk, dressed in an old t-shirt and worn jeans, carrying a battered leather jacket that looked too big for him and a small backpack.

"None of your business."

"I was only asking."

"Well, don't."

She typed a few buttons and sat back in her chair, looking like the cat that got the cream. Aaron came around and peered over her shoulder.

"Are you downloading a virus?"

"Yes…and I've sent some particularly nasty files to some journalists I know."

"A virus could shut down the whole system." He gasped.

"That's the plan. It will also wipe out all their records, and when they do to do a back-up, this particular virus will take out that as well."

"Clever," he said, impressed.

"Not really."

A screen message popped up to tell her the upload was finished. Izzy removed the memory stick and stood up, forcing Aaron to quickly get out of the way. She slipped the stick in a pocket in her trousers and made for the door.

"You off, then?" he asked, a hint of desperation in his voice.

Izzy didn't answer, instead she opened the door leading down into the next floor. She did not hear what the boy said next and was just about to descend when he shouted: "Hey! I'm asking you a question."

"What?" She turned around. He was standing, his face a picture of concern, at the top of the stairs.

"Will you take me with you?"

"I don't take on extra baggage. Why would you want to come with me anyway? You know what I did" Izzy stared at this strange boy. He was not afraid of her anymore. He should have been, but he was not. He nodded hopefully. She shook her head "I just can't. I'm sorry."

"Please, I'm begging. My pimp will have my guts for garters when he finds out old Fleming is dead. He'll blame me. He was one of his best customers." Was he actually holding his hands up in prayer?

"Well, it's hardly your fault," she replied, ignoring his pleading eyes.

"He'll still blame me and beat me senseless for it!" he said. "Please! Let me come. I don't want this life. I never wanted it. They force me to work for them." Tears misted his eyes, and his voice choked. "I just want to go home."

"And where's home?" Why was she even getting involved? This boy meant nothing to her.

"Glasgow. That's where you're from, isn't it?"

She was silent. Thinking.

"He'll beat me and make me go with other men. I can't take it anymore. Please." The boy sounded desperate now and something inside her relented. She couldn't leave this poor, undernourished boy to be pimped out to the highest bidder. Despite her best attempt not to feel pity for him, she knew she had to help.

"Fine, you can come with me." Izzy sighed. A smile broke across Aaron's face. "I'll take you to Glasgow, but then that's it. You're on your own. Got it?"

He nodded. "Cool." She motioned for the boy to follow her downstairs. He picked up his bag and trotted after her.

"Stay close to me, ask me no questions and we'll get on alright," she said, leading him to the rear of the property where another stairwell took them to the basement exit. "And for God's sake, stop smiling. It's off-putting."

"Sorry."

****

The back alley was quiet and dark when they crept up the external stairs from the basement to get to street level. The sounds of the city seemed muted here, and Izzy was relieved to have got out of the house without being seen. After securing the house again, she took Aaron across a small courtyard to a rear gate that she had left ajar for ease of escape. Slowly she pulled it open and looked left out into the cobbled alleyway. She turned to look right and jumped. There was a large man standing in the shadows on the opposite side of the narrow lane. She quickly pulled her head back inside.

"We've got company," she whispered to Aaron.

"Who is it? Did he see you?" He walked up to the gate and peeped out. "Oh shit!" he gasped, immediately coming back inside the safety of the courtyard.

"What? Do you know him?"

"That's Al Grosvenor," he said, hurrying to hide behind her. "He works for my pimp! He must be waiting for me."

Izzy turned around to get a look at him and, in the faint light of the moon, could see that the boy was terrified.

"Why would he be waiting for you when you said you were normally with Fleming all night?"

"I might have a history of trying to escape," he confessed, "but I didn't know Al would be here, honest. I would never have come this way if I thought… Can you kill him?"

She smiled. This kid had spirit and she liked that.

"I can, but I'll not. It's too messy," she replied. "Okay, leave this to me." She grabbed his arm. "Keep behind me and don't make eye contact."

Al Grosvenor was a tall, heavy-set man, with a shaved head and a growling face. He immediately stepped forward when she and Aaron exited the property.

"Stop!" he snarled as Izzy and the boy began to walk away from him. "You've got something that doesn't belong to you!"

Izzy stopped, slowly turned around and looked up to the man. She was tall, but he was a good head taller.

"Are you speaking to me?"

"I don't see anyone else here, do you?" His voice was rasping and he was giving her a menacing look. "Take your hands off the boy."

"Who, him?" she said, not letting go of Aaron, and pointing at him with her free hand. "I'm afraid there's been some mistake. This boy is with me.

"Aaron!" Al said, ignoring her. "Get over here, boy! Now!"

Aaron shook his head and stayed rooted to the spot.

"I said…come here!" Al took a step forward, causing Aaron to whimper and jump behind the safety of the assassin.

"He's not going to come with you," Izzy snarled. "So, why don't you just fuck off and crawl back into the sewer you slithered out of?"

In the light of the dimly lit alleyway, the man grinned. "Oh, it's going to be like that, is it?" he said, lacing his fingers together and giving them a good crack.

Izzy winced. She hated it when people did that. Al took a step forward, fist up ready to punch Izzy. The assassin let go of Aaron, pushed him out of the way and leapt into battle. Using her foot, she swiped Al, sending the big man crashing to the ground. Before he could get up again, before he was barely aware he was down, she was on him, punching the living daylights out of him until his face was bloodied, and finally he slumped into unconsciousness. Only then did Izzy stop punching. She wiped her gloved hands on Al's sweatshirt and stood up.

"I bloody hate it when people crack their fingers," she muttered as she re-joined a stunned Aaron. The boy's face shone with fresh respect.

"You are crazy!" he said, "but brilliant crazy."

"I know!" she said. "Now come on. We've got a train to catch."

Chapter 4 - It Can't Be Him!

They took the sleeper from Euston Station and arrived in Glasgow's Central Station just after seven the following morning. The old Victorian station was busy with other rail users, staff and the dirty grey pigeons that wandered the old sandstone, iron and glass building, searching for food. The pair got themselves quickly through the electronic ticket barriers before coming to a stop underneath the old station clock.

The large Victorian clock had, for more than 150 years, been the meeting place for Glaswegians seeking romance. Many a love story had begun under that clock, but it was for goodbyes that it was used that day. Izzy turned to Aaron who suddenly looked lost and lonely. His face was flushed, and he seemed to be finding it hard to look at her. There was an air of sadness about the boy. Izzy steeled herself. She couldn't let herself get involved any further. That wouldn't do. She had done her bit, had brought him back to Scotland, safe and sound. He was someone else's problem now.

"So, are you going to be okay from here?" she asked, watching his face to see if he was going to tell her the truth.

"Yes." Aaron gave her a weak smile.

"Hmmm. Alright." Izzy had to take his word for it. She had

to be professional about this. She couldn't afford to get emotionally involved. "Well, it's been nice meeting you, Aaron..."

"You too."

"...and remember...?"

"I never saw you."

"Correct," she answered with a smile. "Well, have a good life, keep out of trouble and get yourself a decent job," she added, not sure why she was caring. "Goodbye."

"Bye."

The assassin started to walk away, but stopped immediately when she heard him call out to her. She turned around.

"Thanks for getting me home and getting me away from... you know!" he shouted. "I really appreciate it. Everything you've done and that. You're a lifesaver!"

"You're welcome, Aaron," she replied, smiling at the irony. Izzy was about to resume her walk to the car park when something about the boy's troubled face stopped her. She looked at him quizzically then re-joined him under the ornate old clock.

"You do have a home to go to, don't you?" she asked, watching for his reaction.

"Aye, of course." He said it with some conviction, but she was not convinced.

"Aaron, why did you leave Glasgow in the first place? What made you leave your family and friends and go to London?" Under her piercing gaze, he suddenly looked very young and very, very uncomfortable. He would not look her in the eye. "Aaron?"

He looked up. Bit his lip. She knew see he was deciding which part of the truth to tell her, if at all.

"Well?"

He said nothing.

"Look, if you're not going to tell me the truth, there is no point me standing around here like an idiot. I've got too much to do." Izzy turned on her heel and started to slowly walk away. One…two…three…she counted inwardly.

"Wait!" he called.

She stopped and turned around again.

"Okay, I left because it wasn't good back home," he said, walking towards her. "My maw's a junkie and my da's dead. She lives with an arsehole called Shuggie who's handy with his fists. That's why I left. I went to London 'cos I thought I could get a job down there. And I did, sort of." He looked away, his face burning with embarrassment.

"So, can you go back to your mum's house?"

He shrugged.

"What does that mean?" she asked, imitating his shrug. "You can or you can't?"

He shrugged again. Then shook his head.

"So, you don't actually have a home to go back to?"

"No."

"So, what were you going to do when we got back to Glasgow? Where were you planning to go?"

He shrugged. "Dunno. Sleep rough, I suppose."

She rolled her eyes and thought for a moment. Then she pursed her lips, all the time looking at the young lad standing before her. Should she take him back with her? She had the room, and he would be safe there. She chewed on her bottom lip.

"Okay," she said with conviction.

Hope blossomed in Aaron's eyes. "What?"

"Okay, you can come back with me," she said. "I've got a spare room you can have until you get on your feet."

"Do you mean that? Thank you!" He put his arms out to give her a hug, but she shied away.

"I don't hug, never hug me," she said, then continued: "It's room and board only, and you'll need to muck in around the house. We all muck in. And, you should know: I don't hold sway with drugs or drink. They're banned. Got me? And you will never, never interfere with or ask about my work. Okay?"

"Yeah."

"And we'll have to get you some new clothes," she added, inspecting at his shabby t-shirt and jeans. "But that can wait. Come on."

****

Izzy's car was parked in the station's underground car park. A top-of-the-range 4X4, it was immaculate inside and sported a fancy music player. As soon as he got in the car and without asking permission, Aaron leant over and switched it on. They were blasted by the over excitable voice of a local radio announcer talking about some nonsense to do with a celebrity. Izzy grimaced and immediately switched it off.

"Oh, come on! Let's get some tunes on!" he whined.

"Sure." She took out her cell phone, clicked a few buttons and the soothing sound of soft jazz washed over them.

"I was thinking something more modern than that," he said, putting on his seatbelt and crossing his arms in disgust.

"My car, my rules, my music." Izzy started the engine.

"Hmphfff." Huffing, Aaron stared out the window.

Izzy navigated out of the narrow confines of the car par and soon they were heading up Bath Street in the direction of the city's cosmopolitan west-end. As they drove, Aaron pointed out various landmarks along the way, asking her the names of buildings he did not know. They drove past the Kelvingrove Museum

& Art Gallery and the old Transport Museum before heading up Byres Road to join Great Western Road.

Izzy could have joined the M8 motorway and driven south over the city's Kingston Bridge towards Paisley. The motorway then looped around to the Erskine Bridge, taking her back north over the River Clyde. It seemed like a crazy way to go, but was actually quicker.

She, however, preferred a slower pace of driving. It was her way of unwinding, which was why she'd opted for this route.

At the top of Byres Road, Izzy turned left and followed the A82, also known as Great Western Road, as it took them through Hyndland, Anniesland and Drumchapel. They soon left Glasgow's borders, travelling further west past the towns of Clydebank and Dumbarton. The traffic was heavy, and the constant stress of it made Izzy irritable. At least Aaron had gone quiet. The boy was too busy taking in the urban scenery around him to bother with words.

At last, they freed themselves of the traffic around Dumbarton and made their way towards the road that snaked around Loch Lomond.

"Oh wow!" said Aaron, as the loch and mountains came into view. "This is amazing."

"Haven't you been here before?"

"No, never."

It was the first time that Izzy had seen him look so happy in the short time she had known him and assuaged her fear that she was doing the wrong thing by taking him with her. All the way from Glasgow, a nagging doubt had filled her head as to whether she could look after this wayward teen. In the past, she had only taken in troubled adults and only those she had a previous connection with, but Aaron was a special case. She cursed her soft heart. Izzy should get one of the team to look into his background, check his story about the abusive family. For all she knew, he was spinning her a line to gain her confidence to rob her or something.

Izzy glanced at Aaron and saw the wonder in the boy's face. He was loving the stunning view of the loch and surrounding mountains. Although her brain was telling her to be careful, her gut instinct was that this was a good kid and she should help him.

They were about halfway up the loch, on the western side, when Izzy slowed the car down and took a left turn on to a farm track. She stopped the car at a metal farm gate and got out. There was nothing unusual about the gate, except for a small metal box mounted on a metal post to one side.

Izzy keyed in some numbers and the gate swung open. She returned to the vehicle and drove it through leaving the gate to close itself behind her. The track took them up the mountainside for a good few hundred yards before turning left into a wooded area of mainly Scots pine. As they entered the privacy of the woodland, the track changed: it was no longer muddy but smooth tarmac.

Aaron noticed this as soon as the car stopped bumping along and questioned it.

"Disguise," Izzy replied. "From the main road the entrance to the farm looks just like a rack, something only a tractor would use. However, I felt, for the good of our vehicles, we really needed a proper road to the farm, that's why I had the tarmac put in where it can't be seen."

The single-track road wove through the forest and halfway up the mountain. From his vantage point in the front passenger seat, Aaron could see the roof of a farmhouse up ahead, and when he turned around, the glittering blue of Loch Lomond stretched out behind him. He turned back just as the car cleared the forest, and the farm-house was displayed in all its glory.

Traditionally built, the 250-year-old house sat between a neat garden in the front and outbuildings to one side and the rear. The two-storey, stone house had been white-washed and had a grey slate roof. It was beautifully kept, and the entire homestead was surrounded by a perfectly built dry stone wall. Surrounding the farm, dotted here and there across the mountain, was a flock of black-faced sheep, happily chewing on the sparse grass that covered it. A tractor was just visible behind a large metal barn, and there were huge bundles of hay stacked inside.

Izzy parked the car at the garden gate. Small, metal and painted black, the gate displayed the farm's name Crann Darach.

"Is this it?" He sounded excited. "Is this where you live? On a farm?"

"Yes."

"What does Crann Darach mean? Is it Gaelic?"

"Yes, and it means oak tree," she replied, grabbing her bag and exiting the car.

"Have you got oak trees here? Is that why it's called that?" Aaron could hardly get out of the car he was that excited. His face was flushed and his eyes were full of wonder.

"Oh, look, there's Tom," Izzy said, hoping to distract him from his barrage of questions.

Aaron looked to see a black and white Border Collie come rushing out of the farm yard towards them. Barely containing his excitement, the dog, tongue hanging from mouth, bounded up and pounced on his mistress. As she fussed over the dog, rubbing his back and kissing his head, Aaron took a step forward, and Tom stopped what he was doing, turned to the boy and growled low and long. Aaron, clutching his rucksack, stepped back.

"Don't worry about old Tom here," Izzy reassured him. "He's actually a big sweetie; he's just wary of strangers. He'll be fine once he gets to know you. Now, let's go inside, and I'll introduce you to everyone else."

She swung open the gate and, without waiting for Aaron, walked along the stone path up to the small wooden front door. Painted black, the door sported a highly polished door knocker and ball handle. Assuming the boy would follow, Izzy went in, shadowed by Tom. Aaron trailed along at a distance.

****

The front door opened straight into a large sunny kitchen where three people were sitting drinking tea. The table was laden with a huge navy-blue teapot and an array of differently decorated mugs. A large jug half-filled with milk and a sugar bowl were the only other things on the table.

At the head of the old kitchen table was an enormous man drinking out of a My Little Pony mug. His head was shaved and he had neck tattoos and a nose ring. He wore a t-shirt tightly stretched across a muscular chest and a dirty pair of overalls tied at the waist. He stood up to refill his colleague's mugs just as Aaron entered.

Next to him was a woman in her 60s with a kindly face. She was slim, petite and busy passing around freshly baked biscuits. To her right was a thin, scrawny man with dark spikey hair and snake tattoos on his bare arms. He gently held a newborn lamb in his lap.

"Aaron, come in," Izzy said as she walked towards the table.

"Come and sit down, and I'll introduce you to everyone."

As the boy scurried across the flagstones to join her, she began to reel off names: "This is Dinghy…" The bald man nodded. "Mary…"

"Hello, dear," Mary said.

"…and Robert," Izzy said. "Everyone, this is Aaron. I sort of acquired him in London. He's going to be staying with us for a while." She put down her bag and pulled out a chair. "You been baking again, Mary?"

"Not me…Robert." Mary nodded to the quiet man with the lamb. She offered her the plate of biscuits. Izzy took one and popped it in her mouth, smiling with delight. Then she remembered Aaron.

"Pull up a pew," Izzy said to Aaron, as she pushed a chair out with her foot. "Don't be shy."

Aaron sat on the chair and accepted a cup of tea from Dinghy. Izzy placed the biscuit plate in front of him – shortbread, her own favourite – and he took one stuffing it into his mouth greedily.

"So, how did it go, dear?" Mary asked.

"Fine," Izzy replied. "That poison suggested by Robert worked a charm. Thanks, Robert. He went down quickly." Robert nodded in acknowledgement, but said nothing.

"Good, I'm glad there were no problems." Mary smiled warmly before turning to Aaron. "So where are you from, Aaron? London, is it?"

"No, Glasgow actually," he said, selecting another biscuit.

"What were you doing down in London?"

"Working."

Mary cast her gaze to Izzy who shook her head. Best not to question him any further, her face said, and Mary nodded.

"So, will you be staying here long?" Robert's voice was weak and wheezy.

"I don't know."

"And where will you sleep?" Dinghy peered at Izzy. "Will he be in with us?"

"Hey, stop interrogating the boy!" Izzy admonished, grinning. "There will be plenty of time to find out more about Aaron later."

The boy visibly relaxed and took another bit of shortbread.

"I suppose you're wondering how we all got together?" Izzy said. He nodded. They were an eclectic bunch of people. "Well," Izzy began, "Mary, here, has been like a second mother to me. She took me in after…" Her voice trailed off, but she quickly composed herself. "…after my brother, Frank, was killed. Dinghy is Mary's brother, who came to us because he was having problems with drugs and needed help, and Robert…"

"Izzy was the only one who helped me after I came out," Robert interrupted.

"Came out from where?" Aaron asked, eyes as wide as saucers.

"From jail, son," Robert replied.

"What did you do?"

"I killed a man in a bar fight. I was drunk, he came at me and…well, it was manslaughter, but it doesn't help me feel any less guilty." Robert stroked the lamb. "Izzy's been good enough to give me a home and a job here. Me and Dinghy look after the animals."

"So, you are all like me, then?" Aaron said. "Someone who needed help?"

There was a general consensus around the table then the room went quiet. Izzy broke the spell by standing up, causing the chair to grind loudly on the old tiled floor. "Right, I'd better get on," she said. "I suppose I should show you where you'll be sleeping first…now that you're joining our merry band." She nodded to Aaron to rise too. Reluctantly, the boy did as he was told.

"See you later, Aaron," Robert said, gently stroking the lamb's head. It bleated softly.

****

Izzy took Aaron out of the kitchen into a wide hallway. On the right was a wooden stairwell and to the left what looked like the farm's front door. It was here that Aaron paused, looking unsure and nervous.

"Are you okay?" Izzy asked.

"Yeah," he replied, but he didn't seem like it.

"If you're worried that you'll be bunking in with Robert and Dinghy, don't," she said. "I wouldn't do that to you. They are great guys, but snore like pigs. There's a spare room right next to mine and you can have that. It's just a box room, nothing special, but it'll be warm and comfortable."

"Where do the rest of them sleep?" He followed her upstairs.

"Mary has a room in the farm house, across from you and me, and Robert and Dinghy sleep in the old barn. I converted it to additional housing a couple of years ago. It's got a proper kitchen and bathroom, but they prefer to eat with us. They only really sleep there."

Izzy opened a door and showed him into a small room with a single bed in one corner and a large bookcase full of assorted volumes in the other. A fireplace dominated the other wall opposite a large window looking out on to the rear of the property. Aaron took it all in and smiled.

"Okay, so this is your bed," Izzy said, not knowing why she was stating the obvious. "That doorway over there is a small closet. I know you only have the clothes you arrived in, but don't worry, I'll soon sort that out. And help yourself to the books. I only ask that you look after them and put them back when you've finished. That's it. Everything else you need to know you'll pick up as you go along."

"This is brilliant," he said. "I've never had my own room before. It's really nice."

"Okay, well, I'll leave you to get settled in."

****

After lunch, an exhausted Aaron went to lie down in his new room, tired out from the stresses and strains of the previous day. Izzy checked that he was sleeping before tip-toeing up to her study on the second floor, leaving Mary to organise that day's dish washing rota. Her study was in an old attic bedroom at the front of the farmhouse. A large antique desk took up much of the space in the centre of the room, on which sat a desktop computer. Behind the desk was a leather office chair, and either side—from floor to ceiling and wall to wall—were wooden shelves laden with books of all shapes and sizes.

Izzy had always been a bookworm, books comforted her, they got her through the trauma of being orphaned young and being brought up in care. They helped her get over Frank's death. Izzy entered the study, her stockinged feet sinking into the shag pile carpet. The room was warm and smelled of furniture polish. Mary must have been in cleaning.

Izzy ran one hand along a bookshelf, looking longingly at the tomes she had purchased, but not read yet. Nope, she couldn't pick one up today. She was too busy. The first thing she had to do was check her messages, then she would have to have a think about Aaron and his situation. He was old enough to make his own decisions about where he would live, but surely she should let his family know he was back in Scotland. Someone must be worried about the boy.

Izzy sat down on her chair and switched on the computer. It pinged into life. Typing quickly on her keyboard, she opened up her emails to check for new messages. Izzy had not wanted to contact SOS HQ en route home, especially with a teenager in tow. He'd already asked too many questions, and she could not tell him about the Sisters. The organisation was a secret, after all.

There were two messages from Wrath, the first being a generic message that she had sent out to all the girls, telling them about things were going to be done now that Mother was dead. Wrath had temporarily taken over the role and a new Mother would be announced soon. She continued with an update on the Conexus building, hinting that there were changes being made. In the meantime, she continued, there are still jobs to be done and money to be made.

Wrath's second message was a private one, purely for Envy. She told she had a job for her that was a bit more involved than usual, which was why she hadn't posted it on the dark web. This one was for the son of an old friend of Mother's. He's paying well for this job, Envy, so he needs it done quickly, she wrote. It involved child slavery and some very nasty people. Wrath finished the message with a phone number and the name, Adam Harrison. Izzy's stomach lurched dangerously, bile burning the back of her throat.

"No! It can't be him!"

Chapter 5 - Adam

"What the fuck?" Izzy muttered, sitting back and staring at the flickering computer screen for a few moments. It was impossible. There were loads of Adam Harrisons. This one couldn't be him. Could it? Not her ex!

They had been together for a year before Adam decided he did not want to continue in their relationship. He had ditched her by text only months after Frank's death, and disappeared abroad leaving her utterly heartbroken. He had cut off all communication, so she never knew why he had suddenly left. She thought back to her time with him, and pain pierced her heart.

Adam had been her first love. She had only been 23 and shad fallen hard. It had taken her two years to get over him and a further three to stop wincing every time she heard the name Adam. No, this couldn't be the same man. It must be a coincidence. She picked up her cell phone and dialled the number.

"Hello?" his voice was the same—deep and mellow in tone. Her heart leapt into her mouth. She took a breath and steadied her nerves.

"Adam Harrison?"

"Yes?"

Fuck, fuck, fuckity, fuck! Drawing in a steadying breath,

Izzy forced herself to keep her head in the game. "My name's is Envy, and I believe you have a job for me?"

****

Izzy stood near the Land Rover on the edge of Loch Lomond and watched five white swans sail by. She had arranged to meet Adam near Luss jetty and was irritated he was already late. The small and perfect loch-side village was only a few minutes' drive away, so was ideal for the meet. Normally, she would have gone alone. She could more than handle herself, but hearing Adam's voice had cut her to the core, and she had brought along back-up for emotional support.

She leant against the car, growing increasingly more irritated about the sound of the muffled drum and bass music that Dinghy and Aaron were listening to inside. She knocked the window and mimed to them to turn it down. It was spoiling the beautiful tranquillity of the place and giving her a headache. Dinghy gave her the thumbs up, and the music quietened. She breathed a sigh of relief.

Luss was a beautiful little stone village on the banks of the loch and a real tourist attraction, but Izzy rarely came here. It was always packed with people and today was no different, despite it being November. At least the rain had stayed off, she thought, as she squinted up at the grey sky.

"I'm going down to jetty," Izzy said, opening the car door. "Keep an eye out for Mr Harrison."

"No probs, boss," Dinghy replied.

Izzy sauntered up the wooden jetty and stood watching the waves lap gently against the shore. She had been there less than five minutes when she saw a large, gun metal grey 4X4, the driver obscured by tinted windows, negotiating the crowds of people. It drove to the jetty, the engine was cut, the door opened and what Izzy later described as a Greek God in Ray-Ban Wayfarer sunglasses, disembarked from the car. He was more than six feet tall, dark-haired, tanned and had a killer smile. His leather aviator jacket over a white t-shirt perfectly showed off his toned body, and a pair of well-worn jeans hugged his bum beautifully. A leather laptop bag was slung over one shoulder.

Fuck, it is him. Izzy felt herself go weak at the knees as her exstrode towards her, hand outstretched to shake. Pull yourself together, girl, she told herself as she returned the gesture. They shook.

"Izzy?" He removed his sunglasses to reveal a pair of gorgeous green eyes. Izzy felt her legs go. "I can't believe it."

"Hello, Adam." Hold it together, woman.

"You look amazing." Adam gave her an appreciative once over.

"Thanks, so do you."

Her stomach was doing back flips, and she felt like she was going to puke. Her first love was standing before her, all gorgeous and…and…happy. Why was he happy? He should be old and shrivelled up from wanting her. He leant in and gave her a hug. She inhaled his scent. His aftershave was just…delicious.

"Long time, no see," he said, releasing her. All she could do was give him a weak smile. "I can't believe it, Iz, after all this time. I'm glad it's you who's going to help me."

"I haven't agreed to do anything yet." Even she was surprised by the steely tone. Did he just flinch? She looked at him, and the old feelings came flooding back. Could she really work with this man and be professional? She bit her lip. "In fact, I'm wondering if this is such a good idea. We've got a lot of history, and actually, when I really think about it, I'm not sure this job is right for me. I'm sorry to have wasted your time."

She turned and began to hurry down the jetty. It was not like her to pass up on a lucrative job like this, but she just couldn't.

"Izzy, wait!" He ran after her and grabbed her arm. As they touched, Izzy felt an electric shock course through her. She could not look at him. "I know our break up hit you bad," he said, "and I'm so very sorry, I could have been better. I was young and stupid, and didn't think of your feelings. I could have taken the time to let you down more gently, but circumstances... Look, I understand that you may hate me, but I have to put that aside for now. I really need your help."

She chanced a glance into his earnest face.

"Please, there's children's lives at stake," he added, "and you're the only one I can turn to."

"I have other Sisters. One of them could easily do this job," she replied, shaking his hand loose.

"I know, but I want you do it. I was worried about who I was going to get to help me, but now I know it's you, that worry has gone away. Please, Iz, let's put the past behind us. Those kids need us."

Seeing how grave his face looked, Izzy relented. "Okay," she said, "I'll hear you out, but I'm not promising anything."

****

Adam insisted they take a walk along the loch's shoreline. They followed a pathway heading north, and as they sauntered, he told her exactly what the job was about.

"I'm now working as an analyst with the J G McCoy Corporation, who, as you know, is one of the biggest companies in the world," he began. "We have a number of companies across the world, making everything from farm equipment to chocolate. My job basically is about looking at past results and performance, identifying trends and making recommendations… that sort of thing. When I was doing some research into the company archives, I came across some worrying information about one of our companies, Lorenz. Now, I don't know if you know this but Lorenz is…"

"A chocolate company," she said. She loved chocolate and was a fan of their products.

"Yes, they produce most of the chocolate bars in the world. It has 53% of the market share. I discovered a file that leads me to believe the company is an active participant in slavery and human rights abuses at their cocoa farms in Africa." Adam picked up his bag and opened it. "I have the evidence here, if you want to see it."

"So, what's that got to do with me?" she asked coolly, wishing he would get to the point.

"I'd like to hire you to do some investigation for me," he said. "I only have superficial evidence. I need something grittier to take to the police."

"It's not really what I do," she replied. "I have…other skills now."

He stared at her dead in the eye and then frowned. "Yes, you fight for humanitarian rights of indigenous peoples. Elizabeth told me that when I saw her last."

"Yes, that's right." Mother was a big fat liar. Oh God, Mother! A pang of hurt coursed through her. Would she ever stop feeling this way about her mentor's death? Although, what Mother had told him wasn't that far from the truth. She did fight for the rights of indigenous people… by murdering the people who were murdering them. "You know Mother died recently?"

"What? No, I didn't. How did it happen?"

Izzy thought about telling him the truth, but that would have led to more questions. "Heart attack. It was very quick," she lied.

"When is the funeral? I'd like to go. She was a very good friend of my late father's."

"I'm sorry, but it's already taken place."

"Oh!" he said. "I'm so very sorry. She was a nice lady."

"She was," she agreed. There was a pause before she said, "So, the job…?"

"It's simple: I need someone to go to the Ivory Coast to find out the truth."

"Why can't you go yourself?"

"I am going. You would be accompanying me." He grasped her hand, looking directly into her eyes. "I thought we could pretend you're my girlfriend and that we were on holiday. It'd be our cover, and together, we can check out the situation of the workers at Lorenz's biggest farm near Abidjan."

Izzy's eyes narrowed. "I'd don't think that would work. It's lame." She shook her hand free. "I'm sorry."

"I know, but I don't know how else to check on the farms without raising suspicion?"

"Call Interpol and let them handle it."

"I already did, and the farmers hid the boys when the inspectors arrived," he said. "Look, boys are being abused here, and worse. They need our help, Izzy. Please."

She surveyed him. He had broadened out since she'd last known him, but was as gorgeous as ever. A few days away with him might be alright, but would she be able to stave off those old feelings she had had for him? She wasn't the woman he used to know. She was tougher now, less likely to fall for his false charms again. She had never been to the Ivory Coast. It might be fun.

"I'll pay you handsomely," he added. She perked up. Her farm needed a big cash injection to keep going, and she had her eye on a new tractor.

"How handsomely?

Chapter 6 - Abidjan

Adam managed to book flights to the Ivory Coast for them the next day. There was no direct flight from Glasgow Airport, so they would have to first travel down to Heathrow Airport near London and then out to Africa. The Heathrow flights were booked for six o'clock the following morning, so while Adam returned to his hotel in Glasgow's city centre, Izzy went up to her room to pack. It was to be a five-day trip, but she had no idea what to take. A quick look on Google gave her an approximate idea of what the weather was like there this time of year. It was usually hot with very little rainfall, so, she sought out her summer clothes.

As she threw some lightweight clothing into her suitcase, Izzy became aware she was not alone. She turned around to see Aaron standing at her door, surveying the mess of the room. Izzy had taken her time selecting what she would be wearing, opting for comfort rather than fashion to deal with the harsh African sun. Even in winter, the Ivory Coast saw high temperatures, so she chose carefully. The rest of clothes, mainly summer dresses and sandals, she had discarded on her bed.

"Jesus! That's a lot of clothes," he said with a grin.

"I'm going away for several days," she said. "I need all these."

Then seeing his face fall, Izzy smiled reassuringly. "Don't worry, it's not forever."

"But what will I do when you're away?" She could see he was uncomfortable with being left alone with people he didn't know.

"Don't worry. Mary and the boys will look after you," she said. "And it's only five days. I'll be back before you know it."

"Can I come with you? I've got a passport, look!" He took his passport from under his hat and showed it to her.

"No, sorry, it's too dangerous." Izzy resumed packing. Should she pack a bikini or not? She decided she would and threw her tiny black swimsuit in the case. She was going out to work, but you never know she might have the chance of a swim.

"Why, what are you doing?"

"Never you mind," she said. A crushed expression came across Aaron's face. "Look, it's a boring business trip, that's all."

"Are you going to kill someone?"

"No."

"Do you need someone with you? I can help. I'm really good with computers." His eyes widened, filled with possible hope that she might take him along.

Izzy closed her case and zipped it. "I know," she said. "Maybe next time. I need you to stay here where it's safe, okay?"

He nodded. "I can also throw my voice…listen!" He put his hands to his mouth and then from somewhere behind her she heard a man's voice shout: "Stop! This is the police!"

"That's very good, Aaron, but I don't think it's something I'll need…not on this trip anyway. Now, away and see if Robert or Dinghy need help with the animals. There's always plenty to do around here."

He disappeared from the doorway and she smiled. Poor kid, she thought, he must be weirded out by what's happened the last few days. And now I'm abandoning him…or so he thinks. I should really give him something to do, a project. Almost immediately something came to mind.

"Aaron!"

His head was back around her door before she could even blink. "What?"

"There is something you can do for me, if you want," she said.

"Yeah, great."

"Could you do a bit of digging about the Lorenz chocolate company? I'll need some background information if I'm to do this trip properly." His face lit up. "You can use the laptop. Robert has it. He borrowed it the other day to look up sheep ticks."

"Thanks, Izzy." He grinned at her before disappearing again.

****

Izzy gasped as she looked out of the plane window and saw the stunning sprawl of Abidjan beneath them. A large modern city in the south of the beautiful Ivory Coast, it had started out life as a small fishing village, booming following the settling of French colonists in the late 1800s. Now the capital city and boasting a population of 6.3 million French speaking inhabitants, Abidjan's neat grid of streets was packed full of old colonial buildings and modern sky scrapers.

The plane banked in readiness for landing, giving Izzy a perfect view of the shimmering Ébrié Lagoon that flowed into the Gulf of Guinea.

"You know, up until 1980, Abidjan was the capital of the Ivory Coast," Adam said, leaning over her to get a view out of the plane's small window. "And it still has many of the country's government and financial buildings. In fact, the government's lower house still meets here."

"Is that right?" she said, catching a whiff of his citrusy aftershave. God, he smelled good.

"Yeah, the national capital is Yamoussoukro, although many still consider Abidjan the economic capital," he said. "I must admit, I prefer Abidjan to Yamoussoukro."

"You've been here before?"

"Yes, a few years ago after we…" Here, he trailed off and went silent.

She nodded. He must have come here not long after we split, she thought. She said nothing more, deciding to let sleeping dogs lie. Izzy sat back in her seat and prepared for the landing.

The jet's tyres landed with a bump as the plane's engines whined. The plane ran along the runway growing increasingly slower and slower until at last, it was slow enough to begin to drive towards the city's Port Bowet Airport. It was late afternoon, but the sun was still blazing outside, and Izzy looked forward to feeling the heat on her face. They had left a dank and miserable Scotland behind. Now they could enjoy a bit of warmth from the African sunshine.

****

Izzy and Adam got through Customs fairly quickly and, carrying both his and her suitcases, he ushered her outside of the airport terminal. The jeep they picked up from the car hire company was small and open to the elements, but Izzy didn't care. She was tired and just wanted to get to their final destination to freshen up and take a bit of a break. Adam had organised rooms for them at the Baylor Hotel just six miles outside the city centre and reassured her the drive wouldn't be a long one. He dumped the cases in the back of the jeep and, before she could even protest, got into the driver's seat and started up the engine. Shrugging, she got into the car, and soon, they were heading out of the city.

They arrived at their hotel just after 6.30pm. The sun was beginning to set on the horizon, giving the whole place a warm orange glow, and had it not been for the very serious reason they were there, Izzy could have almost imagined they really were a couple on holiday.

The Baylor was a large modern hotel mostly made of glass that sparkled and shone in the evening light. They entered an enormous atrium through automatic doors and made their way to a long reception desk nearby, dragging their cases behind them. While Adam checked them in, Izzy grabbed an information leaflet and read. The Baylor had been built only two years previously and boasted 300 en-suite rooms, two restaurants, a cocktail bar, gym and large swimming pool.

Hmmmm, I might get to wear that bikini after all, she thought. There was also a meditation centre and wellbeing hub. Nice!

"Well, I've stayed at worst places," she murmured, as she watched Adam dealing with the receptionist.

"Yes, it's Adam Harrison and Isabella Starr." She heard him say. "I've booked the Presidential Suite."

The woman tapped on her keyboard and retrieved the booking from the system.

"Ah yes, Harrison and Starr for five nights," she said absent-mindedly. She retrieved two key cards from a drawer and placed them, a form and a pen in front of Adam. "Could you just sign here please, Mr Harrison?"

She frowned as she watched him sign for the keys. His handsome profile just about took her breath away. He seemed to sense her watching him, for he turned and gave her a quizzical look. She shrugged. Then the receptionist handed him the key cards.

"Here you go, Mr Harrison," she said. "Shall I get someone to take your bags for you?"

"No, that's quite alright, thank you. We can manage."

"Okay, so the Presidential Suite is on the top floor," the woman said, "and you'll find the lifts are just over there. I hope you have a pleasant stay with us."

They gathered their cases and walked to the lifts.

"We're in a suite?" Izzy said as she struggled with hers. "Together?" It hadn't occurred to Izzy that she would have to share a room with Adam. However, if they were going to keep up the deception that they were a couple, she supposed she would have to go with it.

"You're my girlfriend…remember?" Adam said. "We're supposed to be on holiday and in love. I couldn't very well book us into separate rooms, could I?"

They paused to wait for the elevator to arrive.

"You could have warned me."

"And miss the look on your face?" He flashed her a stomach-dropping gin. She stuck her tongue out at him causing him to chuckle. The lift arrived and they walked in.

If it's a suite, Izzy mused as the doors closed, hopefully it'll have more than one bed.

Chapter 7 - The Hotel

The Presidential Suite was the hotel's most exclusive set of rooms and consisted of an exquisite interior with an expansive sitting area, off of which was a large, luxury double bedroom and en-suite bathroom. Izzy discovered her worst fears had come true when she had a look in the bedroom.

"There's only one bed," she said as she joined Adam in the living room. "It's enormous, but there's only one."

"Yes," he replied, engrossed in getting the television remote to work.

"But there's two of us," she pointed out.

"Yes, and it has an extra-large bed, so there's plenty of room for both us to sleep without any danger of touching each other," he said. "Ah!" He pressed a button and the tv came on. He began to flick through the channels.

"Yes, but I don't want to share my bed with you." She felt irritated by his relaxed attitude.

"Well, there's always the couch." Eyes glittering with glee, he sat down on it and made a show of making himself comfortable. Izzy scowled. This job might not be as easy or as simple as she'd first thought. She let out a sigh and returned to the bedroom to unpack.

"I want the righthand side," Adam called.

"Whatever," she muttered as she went to freshen up in the en-suite.

You're looking tired, she said to herself as she stared at her reflection in the bathroom mirror. She sprayed her face with a little reviving cold water. A hot shower and a change of clothes were next on her to-do list. Adam had said they would be going out for dinner later, so she wanted to dress up.

Izzy had never been to the Ivory Coast before, let alone Africa, and she was going to enjoy this experience as much as she could. She knew they weren't there for a holiday, but tonight she could pretend. It had been a long time since she had taken any kind of break and, as she wasn't here to kill anyone, this would have to do.

Returning to the bedroom, Izzy opened her case. Now, what was she going to wear tonight?

****

The shower was hot and refreshing. Just exactly what Izzy needed after the hot and sticky day she had had. As she let the warm water wash over her, she felt herself slowly come back to life. It had been long day of travelling..

Ten minutes later, hair washed, spirit restored, Izzy turned the water off and wrapped a big fluffy towel around her. Coiling a hand towel around her hair, she walked out into the bedroom to find a grinning Adam sitting on the bed and eyeing her appreciatively.

"Well, hello, Isabella!" he said in a mock sleazy voice. She made a face and he held his hands up in 'I give up'. "Sorry, I was just appreciating the view. It's been a while."

"Well, don't," she snapped. "I'm not here to provide you

with some sort of weird fantasy or to pick up where we left off. I'm here to do a job, remember?" He nodded. "Let's not forget, we're not actually going out with each other anymore. I'm purely here on business."

"Alright, I was just trying to lighten the mood," he said, standing up. "Are you finished with the bathroom?" She nodded. "Good, then I'm going for a shower."

Izzy felt pangs of guilt as he walked past her into the bathroom. She shouldn't have snapped at him. That was a bit over-the-top, but she hated men doing that—appraising her like they wanted to eat her. Adam had had his turn, and he'd blown it. She wasn't interested in relationships now. She relied only on herself and that's the way she liked it. Big style. There was no way she was going there again. She was single and loving her life. She didn't need a man to spoil what she had and that was good.

A rich baritone voice singing the latest BTS track floated in from the bathroom. She had forgotten it was Adam's habit to belt out a few tunes in the shower. She turned around to ask him to stop when she saw with fascinated horror that Adam had left the bathroom door ajar. It was not fully open, but there was just enough space for her to peek inside.

Biting her lip, Izzy watched as he slid off his trousers and briefs, and stepped into the already running shower. His back to her, what she saw made her body react. A hot flush ran from her crotch to her face. She felt her breathing quicken, and her pulse flutter as she watched her former lover. Adam was still stunning.

Fuck it, he was hot. Just look at that arse!

Izzy watched the muscles of his back move as he grabbed the soap and began soaping his body. First, his face, then his muscular chest and down to his torso and legs. Unable to keep her eyes off him, she gasped as he turned around and stuck his head under the torrent of water. It gave her a full view of the dark curling hair of his groin and the long length and thickness of his cock. The shock of it made Izzy blush, and she finally pulled herself away. No, this was not a good idea. She should not have come. He was still turning her on, and despite her best efforts, she still had the urge to rush in there and have him right there in the shower.

Bugger. Think of something else!

Izzy decided to concentrate on getting ready. Adam would be out soon and she hadn't even started drying herself. Pulling the bath towel from around her nude body, she vigorously rubbed her arms and torso, wiping the water from her pale skin and reminding herself that she was not here to bed Adam, despite his backside being so spectacularly squeezable, but to do a job. She wrapped the towel around her back and with a side-to-side motion rubbed it dry.

Fuck, why did she have to agree to this trip? Stupid woman. She should have known that being with him would bring back old feelings.

"Now there's something you don't see every day!" Adam was smirking at the bathroom door with only a teeny tiny towel to cover his groin.

Izzy gasped and wrapped the towel around her slim frame again. "Adam, I thought you were still in the shower," she said, heat rising to her face.

Adam stepped forward, staring at her intently. His body was perfect, all smooth and muscular. "I'd forgotten how gorgeous you were," he said, eyes glittering. Trapped under his penetrating gaze, Izzy gulped.

"Yes, well, you didn't think I was that gorgeous when you dumped me." Defiance trickled into her sharp tone. He winced, as if her words had landed a sharp blow.

"That was just circumstances." Adam moved towards her, eyes full of mischief, and she held her ground. He ran a finger over her shoulder. The simple touch had Izzy's resolve quickly melting away. Fuck, he was doing it to her again. He was making her want him. Fuck. No way was he doing this, not this time.

"Well, I would have worked around them." Izzy slapped his hand away. "I would have tried to make it work, but you didn't want to."

Adam looked startled. He nodded. "You're right," he admitted. "I am sorry we broke up the way we did, Iz. If I could go back in time to change it, I would. It was unforgivable, and I apologise."

"It was the best thing that could have happened to me," she said, trying to exude an airy mood of indifference. "I've done really well for myself since then." Is that hurt in his eyes? "Now, if you'll excuse me, I have to get dressed. You're taking me out for dinner."

Izzy grabbed her makeup bag from her suitcase, some underwear and a killer dress that she knew would have Adam's eyes out on stalks. She was determined to show him what he was missing. The bastard. She walked smartly to the bathroom and shut the door with a click. Putting her makeup bag on the sink, Izzy stood there breathing slowly in an effort to get back control. Then she pulled herself together. Carefully hanging her dress from a hook on the back of the door, she finished drying herself before slipping into her white lace bra and panties. It was too hot to wear anything on her tanned legs, so she shaved and moisturised. Next came the make-up, the hair and shimmying into the white sheath dress.

Half an hour later, Izzy emerged from the bathroom to find

Adam in the living room sitting on the sofa watching sports on tv. He whistled when he saw her standing at the bedroom door.

"You look great," he said, turning the tv off with the remote and getting to his feet. He was wearing light coloured Chinos and a white shirt.

"Thank you."

"Look, about earlier, I'm sorry I came on to you," he said, walking towards her. "I shouldn't have done that. It wasn't professional and I'm sorry."

She began to say, "That's okay..." but was interrupted.

"It was just you looked so damned good and I forgot what an idiot I'd been in leaving you and...well..." He glanced down at his crotch. "The Beast sprang into action and..."

"You call it the Beast now?" She laughed. Jesus, this man had some ego!

"Yeah, what else would you call this magnificent piece of manhood?" he asked mischievously.

"Oh, I can think of many things," she said. "Are you ready?"

"As ever." Adam offered her his arm and she took it.

****

Adam had booked dinner at the hotel's Lagon Blue Restaurant. Modern, stylish and packed, they could barely hear the live music played by the piano player at the shiny black grand piano on the corner. They were ushered to a table for two by the Maître d'. Situated at the windows, the table looked right on to the hotel's swimming pool area. It was now dark, but the pool and gardens were beautifully illuminated to allow guests to enjoy them at night.

After ordering some wine, Izzy and Adam perused the food

menu, both choosing Ivory Coast seafood dishes. Izzy opted for the marinaded and grilled fish with a side order of attiéké (grated cassava) and Adam boiled yam and mackerel stew. When they arrived, Izzy's eyes lit up. Their food not only looked delicious, but smelled delicious too.

"Bon appétit!" she said with a giggle and tucked in.

Izzy had never eaten such amazing food before. The fish was succulent—flavours oozed out of it and the whole thing went perfectly with the attiéké.

"How's yours?" she asked Adam.

"So good."

They ate their dinner companionably, talking about this and that, sipping on their wine and enjoying the ambience of the restaurant. Izzy couldn't remember the last time she had eaten out somewhere so nice. She usually ate at home or picked up something from a takeaway. This was a real treat, and she savoured every moment.

They did not order a dessert, instead, at Izzy's suggestion, went to the hotel's cocktail bar.

Situated next door to the restaurant, the cocktail bar was quieter, and its blue velvet booths and dimmer lighting gave it a more romantic feel. They sat at the bar and drank piña coladas until Izzy happened to check the time. It was midnight.

"Time for bed, I think," she said draining her glass. "I'm shattered."

"Yes, we've got a big day ahead of us tomorrow," Adam replied. Then he looked at her, his eyes soft and warm. "Tonight was fun. I really had a good time."

She smiled. "Me too."

****

Izzy wasn't drunk when they went up to their room, she had more of an alcohol buzz going, but that didn't prevent her tripping over a chair when she entered the room.

"Ooops." Izzy giggled.

"Come on, time for bed, young lady." Adam caught her before she fell to the floor. His strong hands pulled her towards him, and all at once she found herself dangerously close. She gazed into his gorgeous green eyes and bit her lip, wanting so badly to kiss him, but was afraid of getting involved with him again. They stood like that for a moment, staring into each other's eyes, before Adam broke the spell and stepped away from her.

"I'm going to bed," he said quietly.

"Okay."

Disappointment flooded through Izzy and she felt almost... heartbroken. Didn't he want her? He had wanted her earlier, why didn't he want her now? Why am I even thinking this? I don't want him either! Or do I? Shit! This was all too confusing for her. She turned off the living room light and went into their bedroom.

Adam was already under the covers with his eyes closed when she entered. He had put on the lamp on her side of the bed and turned away from it so she could not see his expression. She wondered if he was asleep already. Izzy stood for a moment, watching him breathe before inwardly chiding herself for wanting him again. Damnit!

Kicking off her shoes, Izzy slipped out of her dress, discarding it on a nearby chair. She opened the drawer of the bedside cabinet and removed her nightshirt from it. It was a thigh-length cotton t-shirt type garment that she had picked deliberately to put him off. Now she was regretting her choice. She scooted out of her bra, threw it on the chair and put the nightshirt on.

"You're not wearing that, are you?" She spun around to see that Adam was now lying facing her with a grin on his face. "It's not exactly sexy."

"I know," she said, sliding into bed beside him and switching off the lamp. "It's not meant to be."

She heard him huff quietly, then he sighed deeply and turned back around. Secretly, she smiled to herself.

So, he does want me. Good.

Chapter 8 - Ferme Escoffier

After breakfast, they jumped in their four-wheel drive hire car and headed out of the city. They were going to the Ferme Escoffier, the Lorenz chocolate farm that was two hours' drive from Abidjan. The largest farm the company owned, it produced cocoa beans that went into their chocolate and sold worldwide. The drive took them through the outskirts of the city where the roads were excellent and then out into the sticks, where things got bumpy.

It was a fine, hot morning, and Izzy had nearly forgotten what they were actually there for as they drove north through the lush Ivory Coast plains. En-route they spotted a herd of zebra almost camouflaged in the bush and heard the loud wail of the forest elephant. Birds flew lazily from tree to tree, and every now and then Izzy caught glimpses of chimpanzees sitting in family groups on branches. It was wonderful.

Izzy could have spent all day wandering around the African countryside on her own personal safari, but they were here for a reason, and she had to keep telling herself that.

At last, a large sign sporting the Lorenz logo came into sight. The farm was only a few hundred yards away, and Izzy found her cosy idyll suddenly became deadly serious. She sat up and paid attention.

Surrounded by high metal fencing, the only entrance to Ferme Escoffier was through a wide gate guarded on each side by two manned sentry boxes. As Adam drove up, a man in sunglasses and a smart uniform with the Lorenz logo on it approached.

"Pas d'entrée, monsieur," the man said.

"Oh, I'm from the Lorenz company," Adam said. "My girlfriend and I were holidaying in Abidjan, and we thought we'd come up to get a tour of the farm."

The man looked at Izzy who smiled and nodded. "English?" he said.

"Scottish, actually," Adam said.

"What?"

"Never mind. So, can we come in?" Adam removed some Ivory Coast francs from his shirt pocket and handed them to the man. He took it and stuffed the notes in his trousers.

"No," he replied. "No visitors today. You can come back on Saturday. That's when tourists are allowed."

"But we're only here until Friday," Izzy said. She tried her most endearing puppy dog eyes, fluttering her lashes comically. "Is there any chance you can make an exception?"

"No exception. Come back Saturday." With that he walked back to his sentry box and stood there silently watching them.

Adam looked at Izzy as if to say 'now what?'. She shrugged.

"Alright, thank you," Adam called as he started the car again and they drove off. But they did not return to the city; instead, they continued along the same road.

"Where are we going?" Izzy shouted over the sounds of the wind rushing by.

"I'm not giving up that easily," Adam called back. "We'll skirt around the perimeter and see if there's another way in."

The perimeter fence was far larger than Izzy had thought

it would be. On one side, a road full of potholes and ditches, and on the other, acres and acres of cocoa trees as far as the eye could see. It wasn't until they had travelled four miles west, that it finally turned north indicating the edge of the plantation. A small track ran alongside the fence, so Adam turned left and parked the car in the brush.

On the other side, was thick and mature tropical jungle full of massive tress with impressive roots and Izzy, who really did not like creepy crawlies, looked at it in dismay. She was glad she had worn her long linen trousers and hiking boots. Nothing was crawling up her legs, not if she could help it. She shuddered, causing Adam to give her a quizzical glance.

"Come on." Adam jumped out of the jeep and grabbed a backpack from behind her seat.

"What are we doing?" Izzy asked, following him.

"We are walking," he said, slinging the bag over his back. "This way."

Before Izzy could object, Adam stepped on to the track and began hiking alongside the fence.

"Are you crazy?" Izzy called. "We don't know what's in there. There could be large beasts, like lions or something."

"Well, you'd better get a move on, then!" He did not turn around, and he did not wait for her.

"Damnit!" she muttered as she followed him. "The stupid, bloody man is going to get us killed."

"What?" Adam asked.

"Nothing!"

In the heat of the late morning, they traipsed for half an hour before Adam stopped for a break and a drink of water. He removed two water bottles from his backpack and handed one to a grateful Izzy. Unused to such heat, she was exhausted and sweating profusely. They sat down on fallen tree trunk under the cool shadow of some teak trees and swigged the life-giving water. The cool liquid soothed parched throats and revived them both.

Sitting there in companionable silence, Izzy surveyed the way ahead. The track had disappeared now and was little more than a barely-there trail. The fence appeared to continue for a good bit yet, and she worried they were on a wild goose chase. There were no breaks, no holes and no convenient gates to break in.

"I think we should turn back," she said. "This is useless. There's no way we're going to get in today."

He nodded and stoppered his bottle. "Yeah, I think you're right."

Just then, there came the sound of rustling. Something moved through the undergrowth. The large leaves of shrubs shook and crunched as something advanced towards them. Izzy and Adam froze. They both looked to where noise was coming from. Izzy held her breath. Just then there came a loud shriek overhead. They craned their necks upward to see a family of King Colobus monkeys moving through the treetops. Izzy's heart began to beat faster. Then she turned her attention back to the rustling, fearful it would be a large cat. The shrub shook some more, parted and a Black-bellied pangolin emerged from the brush and rushed up the nearest tree. They watched as it expertly scaled the trunk and disappeared into the canopy overhead. Adam let out his breath, looked at Izzy and they both laughed.

"I thought we might be gonners there," he said, putting his water bottle back in his bag and standing up.

"Me too."

Adam held out his hand to help her up and she took it. His

hand felt warm and strong, and he pulled her to her feet with ease. She stood close to him, very aware of his hot body and staring up into his lovely green eyes. He smiled.

"I'm glad you're here, Iz," he said. "I can't imagine doing this with anyone else."

"I'm glad I'm here too," she found herself saying. What am I doing?

He drew her closer so that she was sure she could feel the wild beating of his heart. Or was it hers? They stood there, not speaking, still holding hands, and she was surprised how happy this made her. Then he leant towards her and his lips gently brushed hers. He paused. She didn't react. Oh boy! Her heart beat a little faster as she responded. Intense heat shot to her core, sending her knees trembling. He circled his arms around her waist, moulding his body against hers. Looking into her eyes, he grinned and leant in for another kiss. As his delicious lips met hers, she groaned and felt her body go to jelly. Oh, my goodness! He kissed her again, this time with more urgency, and she responded in kind, revelling in his hot caresses of her face and neck. She couldn't believe how much she had missed this— how good this felt, how right.

"Oh Iz," he murmured as he nuzzled her ear. "Why did I ever leave you?"

Izzy froze. "I've often asked myself the same question."

What was she doing? This was not what she had signed up for. She was only here for the money and to help innocent kids, not to reignite her passion for an old lover.

"You never did give me a proper answer as to why you left." She pushed him away and stepped back, glaring at him. He looked puzzled.

"Oh, we're not going into this again, are we?" he said and

turned away. "I thought we had got over this." Everything about his body language screamed exasperation. He turned back around.

"I want answers, Adam, you owe me that at least," she said. Hands on hips, she glared at him, daring him to refuse her request.

"I owe you nothing," he said, stomping past her back towards the car.

"Where are you going?" This wasn't supposed to happen. He was supposed to beg her forgiveness and kiss her again.

"Back to the hotel," he shouted.

"What about the mission?"

"That can wait. I need to re-group," he snapped as he continued striding away.

Izzy rolled her eyes and watched him go. Men! They were the bane of her life. Such big babies at times. Realising she was not following, Adam paused some way away. He stared at her.

"Are you coming?" he asked. When she didn't answer, he added: "Suit yourself. Just watch out for lions and snakes."

Damnit! She would have to comply. Izzy hated being told what to do, especially by Adam, but he was right. She needed to follow. She did not want to become someone's dinner. What was worse, she would have to sit in the car with him all the way back to the hotel. Fuck. She trudged after him.

"Look, why don't you just give me an explanation as to why you unceremoniously dumped me!" she demanded. "That's all I want…an explanation."

He didn't answer.

"Do you know how long it took me to get over you?" she yelled. "Two years! Two bloody years of wondering what I'd done wrong!"

He stopped in his tracks and faced her.

"Do you think it was easy for me to let you go?" he demanded.

"Yes, it was. You did so over a text, if I remember right."

He couldn't answer.

"You said it was over, and that was it. No reason, nothing."

"Okay, I was a stupid arsehole then. I should have been kinder. I'm sorry," he yelled. "But I didn't do it because of something you did!"

"Well, why did you dump me?" she yelled back. Izzy felt her face flush red with anger and the pitch of her voice rose. "I was fucking heartbroken!"

He lowered his voice. "I was young and stupid. I was offered my dream job abroad. I thought having a girlfriend in tow would hold me back, that I had the world at my feet and that I didn't need anyone," he said. "I chose my career over…the love of my life. It wasn't until you were no longer in my life that I realised what a dick I'd been. I wanted to call you so many times, but I couldn't. What I did, how I did it, was unforgivable."

He started walking again. Izzy tried to take in what he had just confessed. What did it mean? Did it mean he still had feelings for her?

"Adam! Wait!"

As he stopped again and turned to face her.

"What are you saying? That you're sorry? That you want my forgiveness?"

"I am sorry, but I don't deserve your forgiveness." He looked at her with large sad eyes and she could feel the ice she had built up in her heart against him begin to slowly dissolve.

She went to him, put her arms around his neck and kissed him on the cheek.

"I'm not saying you are forgiven," she began, "but you should know I no longer hate you."

He smiled. "Well, that's a start."

Chapter 9 - Estelle

It was lunchtime when they arrived back at the hotel and walked inside. For the first time in years, Izzy felt happy, at peace with the world, her mission momentarily forgotten. He had given her some answers.

They went up to their room and, as soon as the door was closed, Izzy took a hold of Adam's hand and gave it a playful squeeze. Then silently, eyes never leaving his, she pulled him towards her, stretched up and kissed in gently on the lips. At first Adam did not react, then with a soft sigh, he let go of her hand, grabbed her waist and pulled her in for a more passionate embrace.

They stood like this for some moments. Then as one and still kissing, they began to move towards the bedroom, banging into furniture and oblivious to anything but the feel of each other's lips.

It was if no time had passed since they had last made love. It felt strange and familiar, and new and old, all at the same time. Kissing her passionately, Adam expertly removed Izzy's shirt as she went to work on his trousers. Her fingers worked his belt, grazing the hard cock straining against the material. She quickly shoved his trousers down over his hips and he kicked them free. Fingers fumbling, she moved on to the buttons of his shirt and soon had it off, followed by her own trousers. As she reached for the clasp of her pink lace bra, he stopped her.

"Uh-huh!" said Adam, waggling a finger. "That's my job."

Beginning with her lips and moving across her face to her ear, Adam set her skin alive with hot kisses. As he moved down her neck, he slid her bra straps down, releasing her breasts. His mouth engulfed one of her hard nipples and gently sucked and teased. Izzy gasped in pleasure as he then focussed on her other nipple. As he was doing this, his hands moved to unhook her bra. He fumbled for a bit before finally releasing the hooks. His tongue then made a delicious detour to her stomach. Teasing his fingers beneath the waistband of her panties, Adam drew them down her thighs. He paused for a moment before burying his face into her, his tongue seeking out her aching sex with slow strokes.

"Ohhhhh!" Izzy gulped, moaning low as she felt his warm breath on her sensitive flesh.

He looked up at her and laughed. Then rose to his feet, took her hand and led her to the bed. Leaving her to get on the bed, Adam removed his jockey shorts and discarded them on the floor. Then he lay down beside Izzy and began to slowly run his finger up and down her body. Izzy trembled with excitement. It had been some time since she'd last been with a man.

"Are you sure you want this?" Adam whispered in her ear.

Izzy shot him an 'are you insane?' look. "If you don't make love to me right now, Adam Harrison, you're going to be sorry!"

He laughed and kissed her again on the lips. His calloused hand caressed her skin, sliding over the smooth curves of hips and back to her buttocks, before trailing over to her stomach and up to her breast. He fondled the taut flesh, kissing her on her lips, under her ear, on her neck. Izzy was floating in heaven as the hand travelled south again. He rolled her on to her back and gently parted her legs. His hand cupped her pubic area, and the fingers went exploring. Adam quickly found her clitoris and, still kissing her passionately on the neck, began to rub gently growing in intensity as she wriggled and writhed in pleasure.

"Oh, that's good!" she gasped. "Oh my God!"

He continued rubbing until she was an inch off orgasm, when he stopped but didn't remove his hand. Instead, he curled two fingers upward inside her.

"Oh fuck!" she gasped, ready to explode with desire.

"Oh my, we are a little wet, aren't we?" he giggled in her ear.

"Shut up and get inside me." Izzy could hardly contain herself at this point, hips arching up against his hand. "Hurry up!" He climbed on top of her and slid himself in. She grunted. He was big and she loved it.

Slowly, slowly, Adam began to rhythmically thrust. The rhythm grew stronger, faster until they were both on the edge of sheer ecstasy. On and on he went. Then at last he stopped thrusting, groaned and gave one final thrust, bringing Izzy and himself to orgasm.

"Oh!" she gasped as waves of bliss washed over her. The pleasure, the elation of the orgasm was almost too much, and it took her a few seconds to realise Adam was staring down at her. She smiled.

"Did you enjoy that?" he asked, collapsing on top of her and kissing her on her neck.

"Way too much." "Did you?"

He stopped kissing her neck and kissed her on the lips. "Way," he said, interjecting each word with a kiss, "too…much…"

She giggled with each kiss and kissed him back. "I've missed this."

"Me too."

They stared at each other for what seemed like forever before Adam broke the spell by pushing himself up and out of her.

"Sorry, my arm was cramping," he said, sitting up.

She turned on her side to silently look at him. She was unable to express how she was feeling right then. Glowing, happy, pleasured…they were all words that she thought about herself. She wondered if he felt them too.

"What are you thinking?"

"I'm thinking I am very pleased that I asked you to do this job with me," he said.

"Me too."

Then he said: "I've missed you Iz."

She smiled. That made her happy. She really wanted to tell him that she had missed him too, but she couldn't get the words out. She was still feeling conflicted about them resuming their relationship, terrified he would hurt her again. Her heart yearned for him, but her head was telling her to be careful.

"Do you know what I'm thinking?" she said at last.

"What are you thinking?"

"I'm thinking I could murder a burger right now, I'm famished!"

"Way to spoil the moment! Who said that romance was dead!" He grinned. "But, actually I could do with something too."

****

Instead of ordering food for their room, as she had hoped, Adam insisted they go downstairs to have lunch. They walked through the hotel's reception area and into the Lounge Bar.

Modern, stylish and packed with customers, the Lounge Bar and Terrace was already filling up with diners when they arrived and it took them a few moments to locate a free table. There were none it the hyper modern bar itself, so they wandered out into the terrace. Tables and chairs were laid out under the cool shade of large leafy pergolas. Izzy spotted a free oneone over in one corner.

As they walked along the pathway, Izzy suddenly became aware of a dark-haired woman in over-sized designer sunglasses off to one side. She was sitting at a table full of businessmen, staring at her. The woman grinned showing off pearly white teeth, stood up and began to walk towards her. Tall, slender, long hair swept high into a glossy high ponytail, she was immaculately dressed in a cool linen dress and handmade Italian high-heeled shoes. As she approached them, her smile widened. She put out her arms.

"It can't be! Isabella!" the woman called in a French accent. "It is you, isn't it?"

Izzy frowned. The woman rushed over and gave her a hug. Then she kissed her on both cheeks.

"It's so nice to see you again," she said, taking a step back, but keeping her perfectly manicured hands resting on Izzy's shoulders. She must have clocked Izzy's quizzical look and removed her sunglasses. "It's Estelle, Estelle Allard. Don't you remember me? She giggled like a child, high-pitched and tinkling. Izzy recognised it right away,

"Estelle? Of course I remember you!" Izzy beamed "I've not seen you since…"

"Oxford," Estelle finished. "Wow, that was a few years ago. So, what brings you 'ere? Are you on 'oliday?"

"Well, funny you should say that…" Izzy began, but was interrupted by Adam.

"Aren't you going to introduce us?" Adam slipped his arm around Izzy's waist and pulled her close.

"Oh, yes. Estelle this is my…er…boyfriend, Adam. Adam, this is Estelle."

"Estelle Allard, enchanté." Estelle held out her hand. He shook it.

"Enchanté to you too," he replied. "I'm Izzy's better half." Izzy rolled her eyes. "So, how do you two ladies know each other?"

"We were at university together," Izzy said. "We've not seen each other since those days. So, how are you, Estelle? What are you up to these days?"

"Are you 'ere for lunch?" Estelle asked. "My meeting has just finished, and I'm famished. Shall we do lunch together?"

Damnit! That was Izzy's plans for a romantic lunch up in smoke.

"That would be great." Izzy politely smiled. Adam nodded.

"Then please join me." Estelle turned to see the businessmen were still sitting at her table, observing them curiously. "Just a minute."

She sashayed towards the table and bent over to speak to the nearest man. Some words were exchanged, the man nodded and stood up. Indicating for the others to follow, he adjusted his jacket, shook Estelle's hand and left with the others. Estelle turned to her friends and motioned for them to join her.

"But aren't you going to eat lunch with them?" Izzy said.

Estelle laughed. "Oh no! We were just 'aving a quick business meeting. I was actually just about to leave, but now I see you 'ere, darling, and your gorgeous Adam, I just 'ave to find out what you've been up to since our uni days." She smiled. "You two don't mind, do you? I'm not being a…how do you English people say…a gooseberry?"

"Yes, that's correct, and you know very well, Estelle, that I am Scottish, not English." Izzy grinned. "Well, it looks like there's three of us for lunch!" Adam winked at her before giving her bum a squeeze. She gave him a look that said 'stop it' causing him to smile even wider.

Their hostess was oblivious. "Let's sit, shall we?" Estelle said, inviting them to the table.

For lunch, they ordered some delicious dishes from the menu. Izzy opted for Gambas du Chef or the Chef's shrimp stew, whilst Adam opted for grilled langoustines. Estelle had a simple salad and ordered the bar's best white wine to accompany the meal.

"So, what are you doing with yourself, Estelle?" Izzy asked, nodding to the waitress who had filled her wine glass. The wine was delicious, crisp and cold . It hit the spot. "Are you still working in Paris?"

"No, I'm working for my father now," Estelle gorgeous brown eyes smiled as she spoke. Izzy had forgotten how beautiful she was and envied her long luscious eye-lashes. "He's been on at me for years to come and join him in the business and so I did it."

"What sort of company does your father run?" Adam asked.

"He runs various companies," Estelle replied. "I think the one you might have heard of is Lorenz, you know the chocolate people?" Izzy and Adam exchanged glances. "What? What is it?" Estelle asked, puzzled as to what was going on between them.

Adam inclined his head as if to say, 'tell her' and Izzy shook hers in response. Estelle looked from one to the other and frowned.

"What is it? Tell me," she demanded.

"You should say," Adam said. "She could help us."

"'elp you with what?"

"It's not how I do business Adam," Izzy said through gritted teeth.

"Well, it's how I do it." Adam turned to Estelle. "We're not actually here for a holiday, it's for business. Look, I'm just going to come out and say it, Estelle, but we believe Lorenz is involved in or, at least, is condoning child slavery on its cocoa farms."

"What? That's ridiculous," Estelle replied with a forced laugh. "I should know because I'm in charge of the cocoa arm of the company. We got rid of child enforced labour 20 years ago. I know this." Estelle glanced at Izzy for confirmation that what she said was true, but Izzy could not meet her eye. "I'm right, aren't I, Izzy?"

Izzy bit her lip. "I'm afraid not. It seems it's still going on. I'm sorry, Estelle."

The French woman gasped, and her left hand flew to her mouth.

"It's why we're really here, Estelle," Adam continued. "We've come to gather evidence that we can take to the authorities."

"But…my father couldn't have known about this." Estelle's beautiful face was white with shock. "If 'e 'ad, he would have done something about it long ago. It's not something he approves of by any means. 'E's a good man."

"No-one is saying he's not," Izzy reassured her, "but we do have some evidence that child slavery is ongoing in your company. As Adam said…" She gave him a hard look that said you shouldn't have told her anything. "…that's why we're here. I'm so sorry, honey."

She reached over and took Estelle's hand. Estelle took a long drink from her wine and let out a sigh. She looked at Izzy and gave her hand a squeeze.

"We must do something about this. You must help me uncover who is behind this. I will give you all the 'elp you need, just ask," she said. "Anything."

Izzy peered at Adam and then back at Estelle. "Well, there is one thing you could do for us. We wondered if you could organise access to the plantation for us."

"Mais oui! I would be delighted to and then you will see it is all a pack of lies!"

Chapter 10 - Koffi

Late that afternoon, Izzy was in the jeep with Adam and Estelle, making their way back to the cocoa plantation. Without even discussing it, Estelle, gorgeous in her suit with a linen scarf around her head to protect her from the sun, had insisted on accompanying them and demanded to sit the front next to Adam. She chatted amiably to him as he drove and kept touching his arm in an over familiar way that made Izzy uncomfortable. She tried not to mind—she knew Estelle didn't mean anything by it—but her former uni friend was being a bit too touchy feely with someone Izzy now considered to be hers. It wouldn't have been so bad if she could hear what they were talking and laughing about, but the openness of the jeep made it impossible to grasp their conversation over the rush of the wind. She sat in the back and sulked, ruing the fact that Estelle was there.

They didn't need her to be there, but Estelle was worried about the welfare of her workers and the company's reputation. She was only too happy to arrange for them to visit the sprawling plantation to show them, as she put it, that it was all a pack of lies made up by their biggest rival, another chocolate company.

As they approached the gate at Ferme Escoffier, they were

once again stopped by the guard. It was the same one as earlier but on recognising Estelle, he waved them through right away and nodded to Estelle as she passed.

The driveway was a straight as a Roman road and led through a plantation of cocoa trees up to the main house, a mile away from the front gate. It was a traditional colonial style house—two-storied, white-washed, red tin roof with large windows and a covered porch wrapped all the way around it. There were also several outbuildings, which Estelle informed them housed storage areas and a processing plant. She pointed them out as they disembarked and walked towards the house.

"And over there is where our workers live," she continued.

Izzy looked to see a couple of rows of long houses that appeared to be in in good condition.

"Can I just say that any time I have visited this site, I have never seen child labour. Ever," Estelle continued as she got out of the jeep. "It just doesn't happen here."

"I know," Izzy said, joining her in front of the main house. "But you understand that we have to check."

"So, what was this evidence you found anyway?" Estelle wanted to know as they climbed the three steps that led on to the house veranda and the front door.

"It was Adam who found it," Izzy said.

Estelle turned around to look at Adam, in a skip cap, who was bringing up the rear. She gave him a tight smile and he nodded.

"Was it indeed? You'll need to tell me more about that later."

As they reached the double doors of the house entrance, they suddenly opened and a tall dark man wearing sunglasses, a crumpled safari shirt and shorts stepped out. He smiled broadly when he saw Estelle. She slipped her arm out of Izzy's loose grip and went to greet him.

"Mademoiselle Allard," he said in French with a heavy Ivory Coast accent, "de retour si tôt?" (back so soon?).

"Yes, I am back rather sooner than expected, but, well, something's been brought to my attention that I'd like to talk to you about, Karim," Estelle said in English. She turned to Izzy and Adam. "These are my British friends, and they have something they want to ask you."

Izzy explained to Karim exactly what the issue was, and the big overseer looked horrified. "We have no child labour here, I can assure you," he said. "Come, I show you."

With a sweep of an arm, Karim ushered Izzy, Adam and Estelle towards the workers' housing. It was a massive building, some 100 feet long and 50 feet wide with numerous windows. Doors in one end allowed access, and Karim led them inside. Neat rows of beds were interspersed with small wardrobes and at the far end, there were doors leading, Karim said, into the washing and toilet area.

"All our workers are grown men," Karim said, pointing at photos of family members the workers had stuck to the walls and wardrobe doors.

Izzy could see no sign of any worker. "Yes, but where are they?"

"They are out in the forest working, of course," he said.

"Could you show us?" she asked.

Karim looked to Estelle who nodded. "Yes, of course I can."

****

Leading the way, the big African guided the trio into the cocoa forest. It was cooler under the shade and the trees were heavily laden with cocoa pods bursting with beans and all ready to be harvested. Karim took them towards a small, thin man who was busy cutting ripe pods from the tree trunks. The man looked up and paused to wait his instructions.

"Adou!" Karim called.

The man bowed to the party.

Karim walked up to him and put his arm around his shoulders. "This is Adou," he said in English. "He is one of our oldest workers here. He's been here for ten years. It's okay, he also speaks English." He beamed at his worker. "Adou, tell these people we don't have children working here."

Adou shifted uncomfortably, but spoke automatically. "We don't have children working here," he parroted.

"Have you ever seen children working here?" Izzy asked.

The man shifted his eyes to Karim who nodded to him that he should answer. "No, never," he replied. "It is not something we do here." He glanced at Karim again, brow furrowing, and Karim nodded. He gave the man's shoulder a satisfied squeeze and let him go.

"Thank you, Adou," he said, then turned his attention to Izzy and Adam. "You see? No children working here."

Izzy glanced at Estelle who looked relieved and was beaming.

"Is there any chance we could take a look around ourselves?" Izzy asked her friend. The smile vanished from Estelle's face.

"What? But why? You have heard what Karim said, there are no child workers here."

"Yes, I know, but it's just to ensure we've done a thorough investigation," Izzy said.

Estelle glanced at Karim who nodded. It was a small gesture, but Izzy saw it. "Yes, of course you may, please feel free to have a wander about," she said. "I shall accompany you. This farm covers several acres and you can easily get lost in this forest." She smiled. "I know this place like the back of my hand. I've been coming 'ere since I was little."

Over the following two hours, Izzy and Adam were surprised to see only adults working in the forest. As Estelle spoke about the history of the place and how her father got to be the SEO of the company, the pair kept their eyes peeled for the tell-tale signs of children. But they were happy to see it was mostly young men and a couple of older men collecting cocoa pods from the trees. It looked like back-breaking work in the hot sun, and Izzy was glad when Estelle suggested they return to the main house for a drink.

****

There were some rattan chairs and a coffee table laid out on the veranda when they got back to the main house, and Estelle invited them to sit. As they took their seats, she disappeared into the house in search of some cool drinks. Karim, as overseer, was out somewhere on the plantation, so Estelle had to find the staff herself.

Izzy sat down and crossed her legs. It was still too hot for her, and she was exhausted from the walking. Adam sat down next to her.

"Well, it seems I may have been wrong." He took off his hat, fanning his face with it.

"No, I don't think so," Izzy replied. Adam stopped fanning and shot her a quizzical look. "You weren't really buying it when that poor worker said there were no children here, were you? He looked terrified."

"I did wonder, but I put it down to him being a bit nervous."

"He was lying." Izzy leaned in, keeping her voice low. "And Karim was making him lie."

Just then Estelle appeared with a tray of cloudy lemonade and ice in tall glasses. She handed them one each before sitting down next to Izzy.

"Oh, it is so 'ot 'ere," she said, taking a sip of her drink. "I always forget 'ow 'ot it is."

Izzy smiled at her. "Thanks for arranging the visit, Estelle. It was really very interesting."

"I am so glad we did not find any child workers," Estelle said. "It would not be right. My father would not stand for it."

"Me too!" Izzy held up her glass to salute Estelle. "Me too."

Izzy and Adam drained their glasses, then Izzy stood up.

"May I use the facilities before we leave, Estelle?" she asked.

"Yes of course," the French woman replied. "Go inside, turn right, and it's the third door on the left."

"Thank you."

****

Izzy entered the farm house and turned left instead of right, opening doors as she walked down the corridor. Searching for signs of young boys forced into labour on the farm, she was instead met with offices, a living room and a supplies cupboard. Where were they hiding them? She wondered as she met another empty room. Thwarted, she retraced her steps back to the toilet. Damnit!

The toilet was basic, but clean. She used the facilities, then washed her hands and face in the sink. The water was cool and clear and felt good against her hot skin. Where would someone hide workers they did not want someone to find? And how did they know to hide them from us? A knock at the door roused her from her thoughts.

A young teenage boy with a swollen black eye stood before her. He furtively checked his surroundings before pushing a dirty piece of paper into her hand. Puzzled, Izzy opened the crushed note and read: Fatoumata 12, Koffi 13, Yaya 11, Drissa 15, Daouda 13, Burkina Faso. He stared up at her with large brown eyes.

"We are here, missy," the boy said in broken English. "Karim lie."

Izzy nodded.

"You help Koffi and other boys?" he asked, eyes darting about for danger. "You meet us at the gates tonight? At midnight? We tell you everything."

"Yes, yes, I will."

"Promise? No-one help us. You help us? Promise?"

"I promise."

"Thank you." He smiled, showing off a row of gorgeous white teeth, but the smile was short-lived. A noise from down the hallway made him jump and his head snapped around to see where it had come from. "I go now," he said before running off down the opposite end of the corridor and disappearing into a doorway.

I knew it! Izzy thought, as she carefully folded the paper and put it in the pocket of her shorts.

****

Adam and Estelle were laughing heartily over something Estelle had said when Izzy returned to them. A pang of jealousy shot through her, and she fought hard not to let it show. This is all perfectly innocent, she told herself as she approached the beautiful Estelle and handsome Adam. Nothing to worry about.

"I think it's time we get back to the hotel," she said to Adam. He appeared puzzled by her sudden desire to go. "Are you ready to leave?"

Adam nodded. "Yes, of course." He got to his feet. "Estelle," he added, "it's been a pleasure. Can we give you a lift back to Abidjan?"

Estelle rose and shook her head. "No, I can arrange to be driven back from here." She smiled warmly at him. "I 'ave plenty of work still to do, but thank you Adam for your offer."

"My pleasure."

Estelle turned to Izzy and put out her arms. Izzy went to her and allowed herself to be hugged. "Izzy, my darling, it was so good to see you again. Let's not leave it so long in future, eh?" She gave Izzy a squeeze before releasing her. "And 'opefully next time it will be under better circumstances."

Izzy smiled. "Yes."

"Au revoir, dear friend, until we meet again," Estelle ushered them along the veranda.

"Au revoir."

Izzy took her rightful place in the front passenger seat whilst Adam jumped in beside her and started the engine. They both waved to their hostess before Adam drove the car down towards the gates.

"They're definitely hiding something." Adam slowed the car.

"Agreed," she replied. "I've got something to tell you."

Chapter 11 - The Plan

S afe in their hotel room, Izzy showed Adam the note from Koffi. She told him about what had happened and how the boy had asked for her help for himself and his friends. Adam was horrified and read and re-read the note. It was all true then. His mouth hardened, and she could see the muscles in his jawline tighten. He took a breath.

"So, you've arranged to meet the boys tonight?" Adam asked from his perch on one of the seats in the living room.

"Yes, we'll get statements from then—I thought I could film them on my mobile—and then we can report it to the police tomorrow. Hopefully, they'll raid the place and get the boys to safety. Child labour is illegal here," she said from the sofa. "They'll throw the book at them."

"Sounds like a plan. Why can't we go in and get the boys now?"

"Because they'll be ready for us," she said. "They'll simply hide them again or not let us in. However, if the police show up with a warrant, they'll have no choice but to let them in, and that's when they'll catch them."

"I'm so glad your weak bladder got us the results we wanted." He chuckled.

"Really? You're making flippant remarks, now?"

Adam shrugged. "Just felt I needed to lighten the mood a bit." He stood up and stripped off his sweat laden shirt to show off his muscular torso. "That's better. I'm roasting." Izzy flushed, heat pooling between her thighs. *Why am I blushing? I've seen this all before.*

"I'm going for a shower," he said, "freshen up a bit before dinner. Then we can talk about what we need to do later."

Izzy fiddled with her phone, trying not to gawk at Adam as he walked across the room all bare chested and gorgeous. *Damnit, why does he need to do that?*

Izzy sat for a while on the sofa, listening to the sound of the shower going on and Adam singing loudly to himself. Then he appeared at the living room door, naked and obviously ready for round two of their love making.

"Are you coming?"

"Do you think it's appropriate that we have fun while these poor boys are suffering?" Izzy frowned at him.

"Well, there's nothing we can do until we get the evidence, and we're not getting that until later tonight, so I vote we amuse ourselves until such time as we get it," he said. Then he held up a bar of soap. "I'll soap you up all over!"

Izzy bit her lip, unsure of what to do. She had enjoyed their earlier love making, but did she really want to restart a relationship that ended so badly? Adam must have seen the conflicting emotions on her face.

"Look, we don't have to if you don't want to. I know it's going to take time for me to earn your trust back."

"Yes, it will," she replied.

"Okay, well, if you don't mind, I'll go and take a shower first. I'll let you know when I've finished," He disappeared back inside the bedroom leaving Izzy feeling strangely bereft. She sat for a moment listening to the sound of his voice drifting into the living room. I have two options here, she thought, I can either shower with him and have a bloody good time or shower on my own and forgo another orgasm. She stood up. Then walked towards the bedroom. She hesitated at the door. Then went inside. Steam was wafting out of the open bathroom door and Adam was singing loudly as he washed himself. She peeked inside and saw his taut body through the shower cubicle. Fuck, he is hot. Oh fuck it! Lust bloomed in her lady parts and, reacting to sheer animal instincts, she quickly got naked.

It's not like I'm falling in love again. This is all about the sex. She entered the bathroom and her body quivered at the thought of having him inside her again. This doesn't mean anything. She opened the shower door and he turned around. And grinned wolfishly.

****

Standing in the large shower cubicle, Adam put out his hand and guided Izzy inside. The cubicle was hot and steamy, his eyes were liquid pools of fire and Izzy's stomach tightened as she anticipated all the fun they were about to have. Grabbing a bar of soap, Adam began to lather it up.

"You're looking a little dirty, my girl," he murmured in her ear. "Let me get you clean." He kissed her passionately on the lips before pulling away.

With a large grin on his face, Adam started soaping her shoulders, moving down her breasts, over her smooth stomach and down to between her thighs. She gasped as his soapy hands glided over her sex and along the tops of her legs. Then he made her turn around whilst he did her back. She pushed her bum into his hands as they glided across them, enjoying the sensation of his big strong hands caressing her. He pulled her towards him and kissed the back of her neck. She shuddered with desire and arched as he stuck his arms through hers and used the soap on her hardening nipples.

"I want to take you from behind," he whispered in her ear as his hands glided down her body. "Is that okay?"

"Uh-huh," she murmured as his clever fingers found her clitoris and began to sensually rub. She pushed herself into him and wriggled her hips against his hardness.

He kissed her on the side of the neck and gently pushed her shoulders forward. He pulled her hips into his groin and entered her. Sighing with pleasure, he began to thrust, slowly at first and then more quickly.

Izzy braced herself against the tiled wall of the shower and enjoyed the sensations he was creating. His dick was rubbing against her g-spot causing her to shudder with pleasure. As the thrusting grew harder, the sensation increased. The he stopped, pulled out of her and turned her around. She pouted.

"Don't worry, I'm not finished with you yet," he said, grabbing her behind and hauling her on to him. She wrapped her legs around his waist as he manoeuvred himself inside her. Then he pushed her up against the wall of the shower and began to pump. The tiles were freezing against her back, but she didn't care. The lust and the passion coursing through her veins were keeping her hot. As his thrusts grew stronger and faster, Izzy felt her pussy tighten and the first wave of her orgasm. Other waves quickly followed until she felt she was going to burst with sheer bliss. She arched her back and held her breath as carnal pleasure washed over her.

"Oh, my fucking God!" she gasped as her mind and body were overtaken with sexual gratification.

She heard Adam snicker. He wasn't quite done yet. Her orgasm had only served to increase his excitement. He continued to pump and pump and pump until he, too, came with a satisfied grunt. They stood there for a few moments, her still pinned against the shower wall, each lost in their own pleasure. Then Adam opened his eyes and smiled at her.

"What are you doing to me, woman?" Adam whispered breathlessly as he nuzzled her ear. "That was fucking amazing."

She giggled and kissed him on the lips. He responded in kind, and they took a few minutes to enjoy the post-coital affection. Then Adam pulled himself from her and lowered her to the ground.

The pair of them showered for real then, helping each other to clean off the sweat of their love making and both stepped out all satisfied and squeaky clean. Izzy wrapped a towel around her body and moved into the bedroom, intending to get ready for dinner.

She was just sorting out her underwear when there was a rap at the door.

Izzy looked round at the naked Adam, who was drying his hair, to see if he knew anything about it. He shrugged so she hurried to the door. Glancing back to make sure her lover could not be seen by the caller, Izzy yanked open the door and gasped. Estelle was on the other side all glamorous in a body-hugging black halter-neck dress. She gave Izzy a curious once over and laughed that irritatingly tinkling laugh of hers.

"Did I interrupt something?" she said.

"What? No, not at all." The rising heat of a blush washed up

Izzy's neck. "We were just getting ready. I've just had a shower."

"Is Adam here?" Estelle strained to look behind Izzy into the bedroom beyond. Adam had closed the door.

"Yes, he's getting dressed," she replied airily.

"Oh good! I was just coming to invite you both to dinner," said Estelle. "My father has arrived and 'e has asked you both to join us downstairs at seven."

"Lovely." Izzy plastered on a forced smile. "We'll look forward to that."

Estelle nodded and then gave her a knowing look that made her blush all the harder. "Well, I can see that you are busy. I will leave you both to it. I will see you at seven."

"See you then!" Izzy shut the door and leant on it. Shit! Estelle knows we just had sex How embarrassing. She turned to find Adam standing behind her, grinning like the Cheshire Cat.

"Who was that?" he asked.

"Just Estelle inviting us to dinner with her father at seven."

"Do you think she suspects anything?"

"How could she? She thinks there are no child slaves there and that she proved it to us." Adam grabbed her hand and pulled her to him.

"Fancy round three?"

"Do we have time?"

The clock on the wall read six. "We do if we make it a quickie." Izzy could hardly argue as she lost herself once more to his kisses.

****

Half an hour later, after another fantastic orgasm, Izzy pulled on a pale pink shift dress and wriggled it up her body. While

Adam zipped it up for her, planting a hot kiss on the middle of her back as he did so, she put her earrings in. They were small quartz and gold studs, understated, but perfect for dinner. She was just putting in the second one when her phone rang. She picked it up from the bedside table and looked at the display. It was coming from Scotland. She answered to find Aaron on the other end of the line.

"Hey, boss," the teenager said, "how's it going?"

"Good, Aaron," she replied. "Really good. Everything okay your end?"

"Yep."

"So, did you manage to dig anything up for me?" she asked, sliding her feet into a pair of sandals.

"Adam was right, J McCoy are paying someone called Bakary Sangare a thousand dollars a month for what's termed 'goods'. When I dug deeper into Bakary Sangare, I discovered he's got a record as long as my arm for everything from petty thieving to drug running and, get this, human trafficking. What's to bet this Bakary guy is kidnapping boys from neighbouring countries and bringing them into the Ivory Coast to work on the cocoa farms?" Aaron sounded triumphant.

"How did you manage to get this evidence?" Izzy was pretty impressed.

"I told you I was a whizz on the computer. It was buried amongst all sorts of other interesting things."

"It doesn't mean they are paying him for boys, though," Izzy said, "but it's certainly a start. Find out what else you can, Aaron. The more we know about how this company operate, the better. But be careful."

"I will," he replied. "So, what are you guys doing? Are you going to kill anyone?"

Shit. She still hadn't told Adam what she really did for a living. "No, that's not what I'm here for," she hissed down the phone. "Right, I need to go. I'll speak to you soon." She hung up.

"Who was that?" Adam spoke up from behind her.

"My…um…assistant, Aaron. He's been looking into Lorenz for me," she said.

"Did he find anything interesting?"

"Well, funny you should say that…" she began. "Come on, let's get the elevator down and I'll tell you all about it."

Chapter 12 - Peter Allard

Estelle was dazzling when they found her sitting at a table in the restaurant a little later, and Izzy felt a pang of envy at how perfectly turned out she was. Dark hair piled high on her head, her makeup was perfect, her nails were perfect, she was perfect. Izzy looked at Adam to see if he found the French woman attractive, but the tall Scot was only looking at her with a calm indifference, and Izzy immediately felt a little better. Estelle stood up when they approached her table and embraced Izzy.

"Darlings! I'm so glad you could join us," she said, pure delight on her face. She turned to her companion, a handsome older man in a light-coloured suit. He stood as she spoke. "May I introduce you to my father, Peter Allard."

"Enchanté," he said as he took Izzy's hand and kissed it.

"Pleased to meet you, Monsieur Allard," Izzy said. "This is my…boyfriend, Adam Harrison."

Peter Allard gave a short bow to Adam. "Enchanté. It's very nice to meet you at last, Isabella," he said. "My daughter has told me so much about you. You knew each other at university, I understand."

He indicated for them both to sit down.

"Yes, we were on the debating team." Izzy took a seat next

to Estelle. Adam sat to her right, and Peter Allard was directly opposite. "Although, Estelle was a far better debater than I ever was."

"You are Scottish?"

"Yes, Glasgow born and bred," she said proudly.

"And you, Mr Harrison? Are you from Glasgow too?"

All eyes went on Adam who looked a little uncomfortable. "No, I was raised in a little village in Perthshire."

"How nice. I've never been to Scotland, but I hear it's quite beautiful," Allard said. He pointed to the wine menu. "I hope you don't mind, but I took the liberty of ordering. They have a small selection here, but there are a few bottles that are palatable."

"My father is a bit of a wine connoisseur," Estelle said with a smile.

"That's fine with me," Adam replied.He picked up the food menu and began to look through it. "So, what brings you to the Ivory Coast, Monsieur Allard?" he asked as he skimmed the starters.

"I'm here on business," the older man said. "And you?"

"Well…"

"I already told you about this, Papa. They were 'ere investigating claims our farm uses child slaves," Estelle said.

"Ah yes." Peter looked directly at Adam who squirmed. "And did you find any?"

"We found no evidence of child forced labour, Monsieur Allard," Izzy interjected. Allard's eyes slid from Adam to Izzy and he appraised her coldly.

"I am very glad to 'ear that," he said. "In the future, I would appreciate it if you came directly to me with any concerns you may 'ave about any way in which my companies are being run."

He leant across the table and grasped Izzy's hand. Looking her directly in the eyes, he said: "Do you promise me that?"

A cold shiver ran up Izzy's back, but she could not take her eyes off his impassive face. "Yes, yes, of course."

He let her go and gave her hand a pat. "Good, that's settled then." Allard picked up his own food menu. "Now I've 'eard they do a very good Steak Diane here."

****

Dinner was over three hours later. Their host had been polite, frigidly charming, and the time had passed quickly. But Izzy couldn't escape the feeling there was something not right about Peter Allard, that he knew more than he was letting on.

"Estelle always did say he was a bit of a cold fish," she said as they discussed him later in their room. "But it wasn't that that worried me."

"What do you mean?" Adam asked as he unzipped her dress.

"Well, didn't he seem a bit odd when we told him about our concerns? He didn't seem the least bit worried that child slavery was suspected on his company's cocoa plantation and changed the subject as quickly as he could," she said. "And then I felt he was almost threatening me when he said we had to take our concerns to him in future."

Izzy stepped out of her dress and turned to speak to Adam. His eyes devoured her hungrily as she stood in her lacy bra and panties.

"I think he knows only too well that it's going on," Izzy added as she kicked off her shoes and lay on top of the bed. It had been a tiring day, and all she wanted to do was climb under the covers and go to sleep, but she couldn't do that. They had to leave soon to meet the boys. "I'll bet he's the one behind the whole thing. Did you see the way he grasped my hand?"

"He's a frosty one alright." Adam lay down next to her and stroked her stomach. "I could hardly get a word out of him all night. If it wasn't for Estelle and you keeping the conversation going, it would have been a very boring night."

"At least that's it done," she said. "We won't have to ever see him again." She paused, then she said: "Estelle was very charming tonight, don't you think?"

"Yes, your friend is nice," he said.

What does he mean by that? Izzy thought. Did he find Estelle attractive? Well, what man wouldn't? Estelle was stunning. And French, which made her exotic. And Scotland had a centuries-old friendship with France. Was Adam planning to make his own Vieille Alliance with Estelle? Izzy felt a stab of envy in her gut. The feeling grew and welled up until it threatened to choke her.

Get a grip! she scolded inwardly. You are acting like a child.

"What are you thinking about?" Adam wanted to know. His hand moved up to the top of her breast and he stuck it into one cup. She felt him playing with her nipple.

"What? Nothing." She felt the flush of yet another blush wash over her face.

"Your face was making all sorts of weird expressions," he said with a grin. "You always do that when you lie."

"No, I don't," she snapped.

"Yes, you do. I know you of old, Izzy Starr. Come on, out with it. What's up?"

"Oh, I was just worrying what will happen when we meet the boys tonight," she lied. "I wouldn't want them to be caught and to get into trouble."

"If we're all careful, they won't," he replied, pulling his hand away, growing serious

She shrugged.

"I would never forgive myself if one of them ended up dead," Izzy confessed. "You hear stories about things like that happening." She thought back to the night she had rescued Aaron from prostitution and shivered.

He leaned over and kissed her. "It'll be fine. We'll be careful." Then he pushed himself back and looked at her, his eyes liquid with lust. "If I thought we had any time, I would take you right now, Isabella Starr," he said, "but unfortunately if we don't leave now, we'll be late. So, why don't you stop fretting, get dressed and join me in the living room in five?"

It took Izzy all of three minutes to pull on a pair of khaki cargo pants and a shirt. She laced her feet into a pair of desert boots and joined Adam in the living room. He was sitting on the sofa checking his mobile. He grinned when he saw her.

"Well, that was quick!" he said. "I'm just making sure our phones are charged so that you can film me interviewing the boys, if that's alright with you," he explained. "I'm going to use their testimony as evidence when I go to the police with this."

"Sure." She picked up her own phone from the clutch bag she had discarded on the table and looked at it. Fully charged. She checked the time. It was nearly 10pm. Shit! "Time to go," she said, stuffing the mobile into one of the pockets of her cargo pants. Adam got up and grabbed the hire car keys from the vanity unit.

"Ready?" she asked.

"Ready."

Chapter 13 - The Meeting

The two-hour journey in the pitch-black African landscape was uneventful save for the odd pothole and the night sounds of the jungle animals. The road, while not the best they had ever been on, was even worse at night. The lack of streetlights or even a full moon made the journey ten times more hazardous and, when their jeep finally got them to the front gates of the farm a few minutes before midnight, an overwhelming sense of relief swept over Izzy. Adam parked in a spot across the road where they could see, but would not be seen, and switched off the headlights.

They waited.

In the sentry boxes, illuminated by dull overhead lights, the guards were distracted in their own ways. One was listening to a radio; they could hear the muffled sounds from where they sat. The other was only interested in his cell phone and did not look up once. Through the gates, they could just see the dark outlines of the cocoa trees silhouetted in the half moonlight. Somewhere, a monkey cried out and a bird chattered.

Izzy scanned the night sky and was delighted at how clear the stars twinkled. If this hadn't been a mission, it would be almost romantic, sitting there with a handsome man at her side. She stole a sly glance at her companion. Despite how dark it was she could see that he, too, was admiring the stars. Adam shifted slightly in his seat and his hand brushed against her arm and came to a rest at her hand. His fingers wrapped around hers, he pulled her hand gently to his lips and kissed it.

"It's quite lovely here," he whispered. He leaned over and she could feel his warm breath on her neck. "Izzy, I think I'm…"

"Shhhh!" she warned and sat up. She thought she had heard something coming from the direction of the plantation. "Is that them?"

Both of them looked at the farm gates, expecting to see a glimmer of light or movement from the boys, but there were none. Izzy strained to hear any tell-tale footsteps.

"No, sorry." She turned her attention back to Adam. "What were you going to say? Oh! Is that them? No…I'm just hearing things."

"We can talk later," Adam said as Izzy jumped up again to see if she could make anything out in the thick jungle that surrounded the farm. There was nothing, just the calls of some wild thing in the distance and the muted music of the guard's radio.

They sat in the jeep for several hours, watching, waiting, always on guard for any signs of the boys, until at last the tribulations of the day finally caught up with them. Adam drifted off to sleep first. He lay back in the driver's seat and his head lolled to one side. Soon he was gently snoring. Izzy watched him for some time before sleep sought her, too. They knew nothing more until the next morning.

****

The sun was just starting to show on the very edge of the horizon when Izzy woke up. Stiff and sore, she squinted whilst her heavy, sleep-laden eyes adjusted to the light. She looked around her and found Adam still gently snoring in the driver's seat of the jeep. He looked so peaceful lying there that she was almost sorry to wake him. But she had no choice. She gave him a shake, and he woke with a start.

"What?" he said, squinting at her through bleary eyes.

"They didn't come," she said, unable to keep the worry out of her voice. "Or if they did, we missed them."

"We couldn't have missed them," he said. "We're right at the gate. Something must have happened that prevented them meeting us."

"Do you think they're alright?" Izzy couldn't keep the panic out of her voice. She was one of the world's best assassins, but that didn't mean she didn't have a heart, especially when it came to helping children in need.

"I'm sure they'll be fine." Adam stretched and yawned. "Well, that's probably the worst night's sleep I've ever spent." He turned the key in the ignition. The jeep roared into life.

"What are you doing?"

"It's two hours back to Abidjan. I don't know about you, but I could murder a hot shower and some breakfast."

"But what about the boys?"

He pursed his lips. "We'll find some other way to speak to them, I promise," he said. "I'm as disappointed as you are, but there's not much else we can do here. They're hardly going to let us in again. For now, I would suggest we regroup back at the hotel to think about our next move."

"Agreed." Even still, Izzy couldn't escape the feeling that something was about to go horribly wrong.

They returned to the hotel feeling dejected and walked up to reception in silence. The receptionist greeted them with a smile and handed Izzy a hand-written note. She opened it and frowned, then looked around the foyer.

"What is it?" Adam asked.

"We might have a small problem," she said.

"What do you mean?"

She showed him the note. "Mary's been trying to get me, but my phone's not picking up. Apparently, Aaron is missing, and she thinks he's en-route here. She says she found my laptop open and discovered Aaron had bought a ticket for himself to fly here," she explained, getting out her mobile. "I'd better call home." She grimaced.

"You can call from the room phone, it'll be more private," he suggested, putting his arm around her and guiding her towards the lifts.

"Oh God, I hope he's not jumped on a plane here." Izzy's brow scrunched as she fretted about Aaron. What could he possibly be thinking?

"Don't worry, he'll be fine."

She wished she could believe him.

****

A cleaner in a smart uniform was vacuuming the hallway outside their room as they walked towards it. Adam retrieved his key card from his pocket and held it to the door. The door beeped open and they entered. Izzy immediately made her way to the telephone which was located on a coffee table.She sat on a sofa, while Adam made his way through to their bedroom where, he told her, he fully intended on showering and changing his sleep rumpled clothes. Izzy dialled an outside line, waiting for someone at home to pick up. Suddenly, she heard a loud shout from the bedroom.

"Adam?" Izzy put down the receiver and stood up, alarmed. "Are you okay?" When he didn't respond, she rushed towards the bedroom door and threw it open. The way was blocked by an ashen-faced Adam who tried to shield her from the sight within.

"Don't go in there," he warned, pushing her back.

"Why what's happened?" She tried to see around him, but he kept getting in the way.

"Just stay out of the bedroom. I need to call the police." His voice was broken, desperate.

"Adam? What are you talking about? What's happened?"

Izzy shoved past him and entered the bedroom. A scream caught in her throat and it was all she could do to prevent it from escaping. A young boy's body was lying on top of their bed, eyes closed and hands neatly folded on top of his chest. He would have looked like he was sleeping, had it not been for the large pool of congealing blood surrounding his head and the jagged angry wound under his chin. His throat had been cut.

Izzy heaved and turned away from the horrible sight. She had seen many horrible things, done many horrible things working as an assassin, but this murder of an innocent made her feel sick. Adam wrapped his arms around her, and he held close until the trembling stopped.

"It's Koffi," she gasped. "The boy who passed me the note. Oh my God! Who could have done this?"

Adam didn't reply, but instead led her to the sofa and made her sit down whilst he rang reception and asked them to report the murder to the police. A few minutes later, the hotel manager appeared at their door and told them the police were on their way. The small man's normally warm and smiling face was replaced with one of anguish as he joined them in their room.

"Where is he?" he asked Adam. Adam nodded towards the bedroom door, and the manager went to look. He returned almost immediately with tears in his eyes.

"Do you know what happened?" he asked.

Adam shook his head.

****

It took 20 minutes for a young police officer to arrive. He assessed the scene, took Izzy and Adam's details, before silently standing guard at the bedroom door until his colleagues could arrive. A female inspector entered the room first. She was a tall woman with dark brown eyes and black hair piled up in a bun on her head. She spoke to the constable first, and then she moved over to the hotel manager for a few private words.

As Izzy and Adam watched, the manager nodded several times before disappearing out of the room. Then introduced herself as Chief Inspector Sita N'Zi and ascertained who Izzy and Adam were. A few minutes later, as she was interrupted by the returning hotel manager. His head poked around the entranceway, and he caught the attention of Sita, giving her the thumbs up. She nodded in reply.

"Okay," Sita said, "Miss Starr, can you follow me, and Mr Harrison, can you go with my colleague?"

Before they could protest, Izzy and Adam were ushered out of their rooms and along the corridor. The hotel manager opened the door of an adjacent room, and Sita ushered Izzy inside. Adam was to be interviewed in a separate suite. Izzy could barely say goodbye to her lover before Sita had shut the room door and told her to sit down.

The assassin plonked herself down on the sofa and waited. Izzy had experienced many hairy and anxiety-inducing events in her career, but this one, where a child had been murdered in her room, was the most stressful of all. She tried to keep her composure, but there was something gnawing away at her insides that just would not go away. Why would someone do this? she wondered as she watched Sita take a notebook and pen out of her handbag and sit down on the armchair opposite.

As a warning to stay away, Izzy decided. Or were they trying to implicate us in a crime?

She heard Sita sigh and looked up to see that the Detective Sergeant was studying her.

"Okay, Miss Starr," she began, "let's get down to this. I'm sure you will want to be getting on with your day. Can you tell me why you are here in the Ivory Coast?"

As Izzy told her the story of why they were there, Sita jotted down some notes. She told her about the suspicion of child slavery, of their visit to the plantation the day before and the note that Koffi had passed her. She removed it from her trouser pocket and passed it to the policewoman.

"So, what you are saying is that Koffi was the one who was supposed to meet you last night with the other boys, but he didn't show, is that correct?" she asked. Sita studied the note and then set it aside.

"Yes, that's correct."

"And you say you and Mr Harrison stayed in the vehicle near to the cocoa plantation all night? Is that right? And you found the boy on your return?" the detective asked.

"Yes."

"Can anyone corroborate this?"

"Well, the receptionist saw us arrive," she said.

The detective noted something down in her notebook.

"And how did you know this boy?"

"I told you…he approached me at the farm. I had never met him before." Izzy was beginning to feel uneasy about the line of questioning. Did the detective sergeant think they were behind the murder? Surely not!

"And your boyfriend, Adam Harrison," she said, consulting his notes to ensure she got Adam's name correct, "had he ever met this Koffi before?"

"No."

"And do you have any witnesses who can say you were parked outside the farm last night?" she asked.

"Well, just Adam," Izzy said.

"Anyone else?"

"The night porter was at the reception desk when we left, he'll be able to tell you what time we went out," she said. She waited until Sita had finished writing her notes before adding: "We went out to meet Koffi and the other boys. They didn't show up. We spent the night in the car before returning to the hotel this morning. We found Koffi's body when we entered the room a short while ago. That's what happened."

Sita gave her a hard stare before speaking again. "Okay, madamoiselle, that will be all for now. I need you to give me your passport."

"What? Why?" Shit, we're suspects in this murder, Izzy thought.

"It's merely a precaution. Please stay in Abidjan until we tell you otherwise," Sita said. "In fact, remain in this hotel until we have finished our enquiries. Is that understood? The management can get you another room."

"Alright," she said. "So, are you going to speak to Peter Allard about this? It's his company that owns the farm."

"We have only your word that this boy, Koffi, worked on this farm," the policewoman said. "We will, of course, follow up this lead, but it seems to me there's little to link this dead boy with the farm."

"But I told you he worked there."

"Could it be you are mixing up this dead boy with another boy you met?"

"No, it's definitely him."

"As you say," replied Sita. She looked at her suspiciously, then stood up. "That is all for now, Madamoiselle Starr." She stared at her. "And please don't leave the country."

Izzy nodded. Shit. She needed to speak to Adam. Now.

Chapter 14 - Oh Shit!

Famished and tired, Adam insisted they go downstairs to the bar for brunch before heading back to their new room for some sleep. They sat down at a table and ordered poached eggs on toast. As a waitress brought them their coffee, they reflected on the night before. Izzy could barely bring herself to speak about the young boy whose body was now lying in the city's morgue.

"We need to get the person who murdered Koffi." Izzy sipped her coffee and winced. It was boiling hot.

"Agreed."

"And I'm going to slit the bastard from groin to chin." There was real venom in her voice that caused Adam to look at her in surprise. "What?" she said. "Don't tell me you don't feel that way too?"

"It's just that I've never heard you speak like that before." He stared at her incredulously. "I never knew that was in you."

"There's lots about me you don't know, Adam," she said. "An awful lot."

The waitress brought them their breakfast and Izzy tucked in. She couldn't believe how hungry she was. In saying that, she hadn't eaten since the evening before, so it was no wonder she couldn't stuff the food down her throat fast enough.

"Enjoying that?" Adam smirked.

She nodded. "Best eggs I've ever had," she said between mouthfuls. Then something behind him caught her eye and she grimaced. "Oh, shit!" She threw her cutlery on her plate. It rattled on the china. She huffed.

"What?" Adam looked behind him to see a scruffy boy in his teens wearing a lime green baseball cap and carrying a rucksack wave sheepishly in their direction.

"It's Aaron! I'd forgotten all about him."

Izzy motioned for the boy to join them and he did so hesitantly. He gave Izzy a weak but hopeful smile. She was not amused.

"What the fuck do you think you're doing here?" Izzy growled. "You were told to stay in Scotland, not fly over here. And where did you get the money for the tickets from?" One look at Aaron's face told her all she needed to know. "You hacked into my account, didn't you?"

"Well, you shouldn't leave bank statements lying around."

"You know as well as I do, my statements and accounts are kept in a safe." Izzy let out an exasperated breath. "You broke into my safe, didn't you?" He nodded. She pursed her lips and scowled. Fuck! Was nothing sacred?

"Well, you're here now, so I suppose you can stay in our suite." Aaron's face lit up. "But don't think you're getting out of this so easily, young man!"

Oh God, was she really saying that? She hadn't scolded anyone like this since…well, not since her brother was alive. "If I were you, I'd wipe that smile off your face. You are in a shitload of trouble."

"I'm sorry," he said, giving her a woeful look, "it's just that… well, it was boring at the farm, and I knew I could be a better to help for you here." He eyed their food and licked his lips. "That looks good," he said, hunger written all over his face. "Can I get some?"

Izzy gave him a look that said you don't really deserve this, then waved to catch the attention of the waitress.

"And some bacon, can I have some bacon?"

Once Aaron had ordered a full fried breakfast and a glass of milk.

"So, Izzy says you're here assistant," Adam ventured.

"Apprentice," Aaron corrected. "I'm also going to be a ki…"

Izzy prevented him from saying 'killer' by loudly talking over him. "Aaron's a bit of a whizz on the computer," she said. "Aren't you, Aaron?" She narrowed her eyes at him, and he took the hint, nodding. "He's helping us with this mission." She glanced at Adam who was watching them both intently.

"In fact, that's why I'm here," said the boy replied. "I did a bit of digging into Lorenz, like you asked."

"And what did you find?" Adam wanted to know.

Aaron shrugged. "There's not much to go on. The company seems legit. The only dodgy bit I could find was about a company called Ivory Coast Security. Hold on, let me get the laptop out and I'll show you."

The rucksack was quickly unzipped and the laptop removed. He placed it on the table and switched it on. Within a minute, Aaron had connected to the hotel's wi-fi and was already surfing the internet. He keyed in a few words and pulled up the website for Ivory Coast Security. He spun the laptop around and showed Izzy and Adam.

"What are we looking at?" Izzy skimmed the screen.

"Well, on the surface, this company seems above board, as you can see they have a lot of top clients, but I dug a bit deeper."

He spun the laptop around and tapped on the keyboard. "And found this man." Again, the laptop was spun around to show a familiar face.

"That's Karim," Adam said.

Aaron nodded. "Karim Ouedrago, real name Karim Gai. He's a mercenary soldier who was part of a team suspected of murdering everyone in a village in the Central African Republic. According to one report I found, he may also be involved in people smuggling, and a journalist who wrote an article about him was found with his throat slit." Aaron ran his finger across his own throat to emphasise his point.

"How...? How did you...?" Izzy was astounded that one so young had been able to find out so much.

Aaron grinned. "I told you I was good on computers."

"So, what's a mercenary soldier doing working for a chocolate company?" she wondered aloud.

"I think that's something we need to find out," Adam replied.

Their conversation was interrupted by someone shouting Izzy's name from the entranceway. Izzy looked up to see Estelle waving at her. Her heart sank. Estelle was the last person she wanted to talk to right now. The French woman, in a beautiful dress with matching heels and clutch bag, was with a group of admiring businessmen, but indicated she would come over to speak to them in a minute.

"Who's that?" Aaron whistled low. "She's a bit of alright."

"Put the laptop away," Izzy instructed.

"What? Why?"

"Just do it," she hissed.

The boy closed the laptop and placed it back into the rucksack which he hid at his feet. Izzy finished the remnants of her breakfast and downed her coffee. She was just returning the cup to its saucer when Estelle sashayed up to the table, all smiles and glamour.

"Bonjour!" she said. She gave Izzy a kiss on both cheeks. "How lovely to see you again! May I join you?"

"Be our guest," Izzy said with a forced smile.

Estelle sat down next to her friend and gave Izzy a concerned look. "I 'ave just 'eard about the terrible murder." She placed a comforting hand on Izzy's arm. "I am so sorry. Is there anything I can do?"

Izzy shook her head. "No, there's nothing you can do, Estelle. But thank you for the offer. We just have to wait until the police have finished their investigations before we can think about leaving."

"That poor boy," Estelle continued, regret all over her face. "Do the police know who did it?"

"Not yet," Adam replied, "but I'm sure they're following up every lead they can."

Estelle nodded, then a thought seemed to occur to her. "They don't think you were involved, do they? Do you need me to get you a lawyer? I can get you a good one. I know just the man to call. What about flights out of 'ere? I have a private jet that is at your disposal. I could arrange to get you out of the country today."

"Thank you, Estelle, but that won't be necessary," Izzy replied. "We've been told we can't leave the country until the investigation is concluded."

"But I 'eard you were the ones to discover the body. What if they think you were responsible? They could throw you in jail." Estelle's voice rose in alarm, causing several other diners to turn around and stare.

"That's not going to happen." Adam dropped the level of his voice. "We're innocent."

But Estelle was not convinced. She leaned forward and said in a stage whisper, "Trust me, they don't do things properly 'ere. Some of the officials are very corrupt. If they 'ave someone they can pin the murder on, they will. It would be better if you escape now and deal with it from your own country. I can help."

Izzy looked at the French woman and wondered why she was so desperate to help. Was it for old time's sake? Or was there something else going on?

When she got no response from them, Estelle sighed and stood up. "Look, I 'ave to go now. I have another meeting to attend." She opened her clutch bag and pulled out a business card, which she handed to Izzy. "If you need 'elp, call me," she said. "Call me at any time. Promise?"

"I promise." Izzy took the card. "Thank you, Estelle, I appreciate it."

"My pleasure," the woman replied. "What are old friends for if not to 'elp when needed?" Then she seemed to notice Aaron for the first time. She nodded before returning her attention to Izzy. "Well, I must be going. Adieu."

"Do you think we'll get the blame for the murder?" Adam murmured as Estelle moved away

Izzy put her finger to her lips and watched as Estelle exited the bar area. She was making sure her friend was well and truly out of earshot before speaking again. It wasn't that she didn't trust Estelle, but her training for the Sisters had drummed it into her to be careful with everyone, no matter who it was. "I think we'd better adjourn to the room to talk about what we do next."

"You're right," Adam said, getting up.

"But I've not finished my breakfast yet," Aaron whined. Izzy looked at his plate. He had wolfed down nearly all of it.

"Well, hurry up," Izzy said. She was still looking at the doorway and seemed distracted. Aaron scarfed down the last piece and put his cutlery down.

"Finished!"

****

What to do next? It was the question that rang in Izzy's head all the way up to the room. They had told the authorities everything they knew, so surely it was up to them to take the next steps? But Izzy's instincts were screaming at her that she had to do something. And then there was what Estelle had said—that the authorities would try and pin the murder on them if they weren't careful. After they retrieved their personal things from their old room, the hotel manager showed them into a different suite a few doors down the corridor. It wasn't as fancy as the Presidential Suite, but it was still comfortable. Once she was sure, the three of them were along, she expressed her fears to Adam and their need to take control.

"Right, now we have some privacy, we need to plan what we're going to do next," Izzy said as she and Aaron sat on the sofa.

"I think we should take a step back and regroup." Adam paced the room. "I don't want to see you and I end up in jail for something we didn't do."

"That's not going to happen." Adam stopped, his expression conveying that he didn't quite believe her. "And wee need to help those boys," she said, rushing on. "We need to get them out of that place before they disappear altogether. Then we can worry about ourselves."

"It's too dangerous, Iz," Adam said. "I don't want to see you getting hurt."

"Oh, don't worry about Izzy," a voice piped up. They had forgotten Aaron was also in the room and listening to everything they said. "She can more than handle herself, I know that for a fact!"

"What do you mean?" Adam crossed his arms, staring firmly at the pair.

Izzy shot Aaron a look that told him he'd better shut his mouth before she shut it for him. He mimed zipping his mouth closed, turning and key and then throwing it away and made her laugh. She shook her head then turned her attention back to Adam.

"He means I'm not afraid," she said. "Look, with all the heat on the company, Lorenz can't afford to have those boys found on their plantation. They'll either move them tonight or…"

"They'll kill them? Is that what you think they'll do?" Adam's face paled.

She bit her lip and nodded.

"So, what do you propose we do?"

"Well…" she began.

Chapter 15 - Biko

From the privacy of the bedroom, Izzy called in some backup from Conexus. She knew they didn't have any stashes of weapons in the Ivory Coast, but they did have contacts who could provide just about anything they wanted. Wrath talked her through who to approach and where. She would deal with the authorities, she assured Izzy.

"And what about the boys? How are you planning on getting them out, and where are you planning on taking them?"

"I know some people who have a charity returning stolen children to their families," Izzy replied.

"What if the families were the ones that sold them in the first place? Envy, you can't return them back to be sold again."

"I know that, but we'll cross that bridge when we come to it," Izzy sighed. "I know some people who can help with that too. The main thing is we get them to a place of safety tonight." The line went quiet, and she could imagine Wrath's face. She wouldn't be overly pleased with the change of plans, especially since it put Izzy in more danger. It was time to change the subject. "So, how is everything going in Rome? Anything I can do to help? Have you managed to track down Dominika yet?"

"No yet, but I've got feelers out," Wrath replied. "The net's closing in. We'll get the bitch, don't worry about that."

"And how are you dealing with being the new Acting Mother Dearest?" Izzy teased.

"What the fuck? Don't call me that, Envy," Wrath growled. "I swear to God, if anyone else calls me that, there's going to be hell to pay."

Izzy chuckled. The Sisters had been through a lot of shit recently. It was good to noise up Wrath. She was so prickly that it was easy to wind her up. "Alright, calm down, I was only joking," Izzy said. "Right, I'd best be off. Got some boys to rescue and some bad people to kill."

There was a gasp behind her, and she glanced over her shoulder to see that a horrified Adam had been listening in to her entire conversation. She held a finger up indicating she'd explain everything in a minute.

"Go for it, sister!" Wrath hung up.

"What was that all about?" Adam frowned deeply. "I didn't hire you to kill anyone. I hired Conexus to find out if there was child slavery happening, that was all."

Izzy turned to look at him and was surprised to see horror on his face. "Did you properly look into Conexus and the Sisters of Sin before you hired us?"

"I…um…well, your organisation was recommended to me by my father and…." He seemed unable to meet her eyes.

"You know what we do, don't you?" She walked towards him. "You know what I do?"

"He never really elaborated," he stuttered as she drew dangerously close to him. They were now chest to chest and she was looking up at him. Despite the sexual tension between them, Izzy could feel that she was unnerving him.

"I'm not the girl you once knew."

"It's only been a few years, Iz, you can't have changed that much." Nerves trickled into his voice. "You're still the scary nut-case I fell for." He waited for her reaction and seemed relieved when she grinned.

"Well, I got scarier." She took a step back. "I've got to go out," she said. "Will you be okay here with Aaron?"

"I'm coming with you!"

"No, I need you to keep an eye on Aaron." Izzy didn't need him going and doing something stupid. Adam wasn't trained for this.

"Izzy, I can't let you out on your own. Not here. Besides the police said we had to stay close to the hotel."

"Which is exactly why I will be going alone." Izzy patted his chest. "I can sneak in and out of here much easier without you two in tow. The police will never know I was gone." She grabbed her cell phone and walked out of the bedroom. "I'll be back soon, I promise."

****

The city's Abobo district was busy with people and cars. Less salubrious than the Cocody Riveria area where the hotel was, Izzy still felt safe walking around. Carrying an empty rucksack, she snuck out of the hotel via the fire exit and caught a cab straight there. She checked her watch. It was nearly 2pm now; she was running late for her contact. Picking up the pace, she walked down Rue 6 and located the street she was looking for. Papillon Lane ran at right angles to the main thoroughfare and consisted of tightly packed, low-rise buildings full of small businesses and apartments. She found the meeting place, a small café about halfway down the lane.

Izzy opened the door and entered, setting off the gentle

clacking of some wooden windchimes overhead. Bilboa's Café was empty, save for a server and one customer sipping coffee in the corner. A tiny establishment, there was room for only three small tables and a handful of chairs. At the back, a small counter held an ancient Italian coffee machine and a cash register. The server, a young man in his 20s, looked up and grinned as she approached.

"What can I do for you, mademoiselle?" he asked in French.

"I'm looking for Biko," she replied.

"Biko?" He feigned ignorance.

She leant over the counter. "Tell him Envy is here, he's expecting me." She slid a wad of bank notes over to him. The young man lifted the money and flipped through it, grinning.

"Wait here, please."

The server disappeared through a beaded doorway in the back as Izzy waited at the counter. She could hear the sounds of a muted conversation between him and someone else, but couldn't make out the words. Suddenly, the man emerged through the beads and motioned for her to follow him inside. She skirted the counter and went through.

There was a small room through the back where an older man with white hair and a large cigar sat in an armchair next to a radio. African pop music played and the older man tapped his feet in time. He motioned for her to sit next to him on a rickety folding chair and watched intently as she sat down. She waited for him to speak.

The song ended, he switched the radio off and turned his attention to her. "So, you're Envy, are you?" His voice was rich and deep.

"Did Wrath speak to you?" Izzy was not one for beating about the bush.

"Yes."

"Have you got what I asked for?"

"Yes, I have them."

She nodded. "And the price?"

Biko took a long draw from his cigar and then slowly blew out a smoke ring. The bluish smoke swirled around his head. "Wrath and I have worked that out," he said. "It's all taken care of."

Izzy knew better than to ask more. "Good," she said. "So, where is it?"

The older man stubbed his cigar out on an ashtray that was sitting on a nearby table and rose. "Follow me."

He led her outside to a beaten-up, yellow van parked in a back alley. Removing the keys from the pockets of his shorts, he opened the back doors and pushed them wide. Inside were small and long wooden crates piled on top of each other. He removed the lid off the nearest one and dug into the straw. Pulling out a sniper rifle, he passed it to Izzy before clambering into the van to fetch other items. He withdrew two handguns from another box, along with smoke bombs and flashbangs. Then he retrieved some bolt cutters and night vision goggles, and handed them to her.

Izzy broke down the rifle and carefully placed it into her rucksack, the handguns and bolt cutters went inside, too, and the flashbangs and smoke bombs fitted perfectly into the side pockets. When she was done, she waited until Biko had finished locking up the van before shaking his hand.

"Thank you," she said. "I appreciate doing business with you."

He grinned. "No problem, lady," he replied. "You tell Wrath when you see her, Biko is her man in Abidjan. Anything she wants, Biko will get for her."

Izzy nodded.

Outside in the lane, Izzy paused to adjust her heavy backpack. For the first time in a couple of days, she felt more like herself: she felt strong, she felt ready, she felt in control.

"It's show time!" she muttered to herself as she hurried down towards the main thoroughfare. Those bastards aren't going to know what's hit them.

****

Half an hour later, Izzy was back in the hotel, creeping up the fire exit stairs. Before she had left, she had stopped the door from closing fully by placing a wad of paper in the door latch. So, it was easy for her to get back to her floor and slip into the corridor. She had met no police officers on the way out, so was surprised when she opened the door of her room to find it filled with them.

They turned as one to face her. Then she noticed the state of the room and gasped. It had been turned over like there had been a vicious fight. There was blood on the sofa and no sign of Aaron or Adam.

"What's going on?" she asked the nearest cop. He was a young officer and was just about to open his mouth when he was interrupted.

Sita N'Zi emerged from the bedroom. "That's exactly what I'd like to know."

Chapter 16 - Rescue

Izzy tightened her grip on her rucksack as Sita stepped forward and frowned. She looked at the bag and then back at Izzy.

"Where have you been, Miss Starr?" she asked. "You were told to stay in the hotel."

"I was in the hotel," she lied. "I was having some me time in the garden. I was reading. A book."

The room showed evidence of a struggle—detritus was everywhere. The telephone had been ripped out of the wall, and the television lay face down on the floor.

"What's happened? Where is Adam and Aaron?"

"That's what we'd like to ask you," the Detective Sergeant said. "We were called by hotel staff to investigate what sounded like a ruckus happening in this room about twenty minutes ago. When we arrived, we found the room to be in this state and no sign of either you or the other guests. Have you got any idea what might have happened?"

Izzy surveyed the room a second time. One sofa had been tipped over, the glass of the coffee table was smashed and someone had thrown several things at the wall, which now lay in various states of disrepair on the floor. She guessed Aaron had been trying to fend off an attacker. There were more drops of blood on the carpet leading towards the bedroom door. Someone had been hurt.

"I don't know what happened," she said. "I wasn't here." But I'm going to find out.

"I would conclude someone has taken your friends. By force," Sita reasoned. "Any idea why this might be?"

"No, I don't know why." Izzy did her best to keep up a concerned and panicked act, while reasoning things out in the back of her mind. Karim! I bet he was behind it. "Maybe it has something to do with the dead boy."

"That's our best guess too," Sita replied. She moved towards Izzy, a look of concern on her face. "For your own safety, I would suggest we take you to the police office where we can guard you."

"No! No, I don't want that. I want to stay here in case Adam or Aaron come back." Izzy had no intention of staying put, but she didn't have to tell the police that.

"But, what if the assailants return?" Sita eyed her warily. "You could be next."

"That's hardly likely." Izzy nearly bit her tongue. She hurried to add, "Not with all your officers here. Please, let me stay. I need to be here in case the kidnappers—if indeed Adam and Aaron have been kidnapped—call."

"Well, in that case, I will leave two officers guarding your door." Sita smiled drily. "I can't afford for another tourist to go missing."

"You don't have to do that." Izzy groaned inwardly. This would make her plan that much more complicated. "I'll be perfectly safe here by myself."

Sita's eyes narrowed like she was weighing everything up.

Her voice hardened, brokering no room for further negotiation. "I insist."

Turning to two of her team, Sita spoke rapidly to them in French. They nodded and saluted. Then, she faced Izzy once more. "We're done here for now.. Stay in the room, Miss Starr. Do not leave."

Izzy did not reply but watched as the woman detective and three police officers left. Two others remained inside the room and took up position close to the door. They watched as she put her rucksack down on a nearby table and began to tidy the room. All the time she was picking up fallen items and clearing the mess, she planned what she was going to do next. Izzy knew exactly who had Adam and Aaron, and she was going to get them back. There was no way Karim was going to get away with this.

If he has hurt either one of them, she vowed, he will be sorry.

Izzy was good and pissed off now, and when Envy got pissed off, you'd better watch out. She finished plumping the last cushion on the sofa before grabbing her bag and walking towards the bedroom.

"I'm just going to take a lie down," she told her guards. "Please make sure no one disturbs me for at least the next two hours."

Izzy entered the room and shut the door. There was no way she was going to get out via the normal entranceway to her room, so she needed to find another way out. The bedroom had sliding doors that led out to a small balcony. Perfect for tourists wishing to watch the sunset from their room and for assassins trying to escape. She slid the door open slowly, keeping the noise down to a minimum, and stepped outside.

The hot afternoon African air blasted her and the sharp rays of the sun pierced at her eyes, but she didn't have any time to think about that. Securing the rucksack properly on her back, Izzy climbed on to the railing. They were several floors up, and she thanked her lucky stars that she did not suffer from vertigo. In fact, she was in her element up here, standing on the precariously slim metal of a hotel balcony.

Next door's balcony railing was about two metres away. It was a jump Izzy knew she could make so she had no hesitation in launching herself towards it. She landed on the outside of the metal railing and hauled herself over. Not pausing for a moment, Izzy tried the sliding balcony door. It was locked. Damnit! Removing the lock pick set from her pocket, Izzy got to work. Seconds later, she had the lock opened and was inside.

The suite was empty, but the bedroom door was closed, and Izzy could make out the muffled and joyful sounds of two people having a very nice time in the en-suite bathroom. She rolled her eyes and crept up to the bedroom door. She sidled into the living room and made for the exit. Opening it a crack, she peeked outside. The corridor was empty. Time to make her escape.

****

There were no taxis available to take her to the cocoa plantation, so Izzy took advantage of the empty valet parking office and commandeered the keys to a four-wheel drive. There were a few in the parking lot, but holding up the key and giving it a press quickly identified the car she needed. The headlights flashed, catching her attention. It was a black Range Rover that would be just perfect.

Dropping the rucksack into the passenger seat, she climbed into the driver's seat and started her up. The car roared into life, and Izzy grimaced. She was already annoyed that someone was using kids as slaves to pick cocoa and now they had amplified her annoyance to anger by taking her friends.

The fuckers didn't know what was going to hit them.

Chapter 17 - Karin

The entrance to the plantation was in darkness. The lights that normally illuminated the gate were off, and there was no sign of the guards in the small guardhouse. It smelled of being a trap and she wasn't fooled.

Izzy drove past and parked the car behind some bushes about half a mile up the road. They would know she was coming, but she didn't want to alert them as to when and how. She couldn't go in the main entrance—no doubt that was booby-trapped. She already knew there was no other way in, so she would have to make her own.

Rucksack on her back, night vision goggles on, Izzy snuck up to the tall wire fence and took out her bolt cutters. She snipped the first wire. The sound pinged into the night, and she froze, listening for the tell-tale sounds of guards coming to get her. Her ears were met with dead silence. So, she got to work and soon made short shrift of the fence. Izzy created a hole big enough for her to allow her entry, but small enough that it would not be easily seen from the road. She stuck the cutters back in the rucksack, widened the hole and snuck in.

The plantation was eerily quiet and that put Izzy's guard up. She had worked in all terrains across the Earth and knew that even at night, a forest still had its sounds. But here, there was nothing—no bird call, no rustling of mammals, not even the sounds of the night insects that normally buzzed. It was strange, and she didn't like it.

Izzy took her time, placing each foot carefully to ensure she made as little noise as possible. The smallest crack of a foot on a fallen twig could bring the whole place down on her. Carefully, stealthily, she made her way into the enemy's lair. She was heading towards the entranceway where she could pick out the sweep of road and, from the safety of the cocoa forest, follow it up to the farmhouse. The cocoa trees would give her enough cover to literally walk right up to it. She hoped. There were bound to be guards patrolling the plantation, and she would have to be careful.

Izzy had gone no more than twenty steps when a slight sound made her freeze. She stood, ears straining and listened. There it was again. A man was talking quietly to another somewhere to her left. She crouched down, watched and waited. A minute went by, two, and she was just about to stand up again when she saw them—the silhouettes of two armed guards patrolling the forest. Izzy could just make out their shapes in the dull moonlight that filtered through the tree canopy.

They are looking for me, she thought.

In the shadows, Izzy watched as the guards continued whispering to each other and realised they were not fully concentrating on what they were supposed to be doing. They appeared to be having some sort of debate. From her hiding place, she couldn't make out what they were saying, but that didn't matter. It was all she needed. As they continued their conversation, she advanced towards them.

Stepping carefully and slowly, the assassin moved with the stealth of a cat about to pounce. She was so quiet, the men did not notice the tall, dark-haired, Scottish woman sneak up behind them. Nor did they hear her unsheathe her knife. She had slit the first guard's throat and dropped him to the ground before his comrade could even react. Izzy side-stepped him as he spun around to see where his fellow guard had disappeared to. Without making a sound, she thrust her knife into his jugular. He grabbed at her and then at his throat before collapsing to the ground dead.

Damnit! Izzy thought to herself. I've got blood on my t-shirt.

That was the problem with hitting the jugular. The warm red blood didn't ooze out nicely. No, it spurted like a broken fire hydrant, the blood spraying everything in its path. She had managed to dodge most of it, but some had landed on her front. She could feel it trickling down the V-neck of her t-shirt. Bugger. Giving it a quick wipe with her hand, she continued on her mission.

As she made her way through the plantation towards the farmhouse, Izzy kept an eye out for any other guards, but there were none, at least not in the sector she was walking in. As she got closer to the house, she could see why. Discarding her night vision goggles, she used binoculars to get a better view.

The yard was fully illuminated by overhead lights and packed with people. Karim and four guards were busy hustling a group of sobbing boys out of one of the farm buildings and forcing them on to a truck at gun point. In the back of the group, she saw the skinny form of Aaron shuffling along behind the others. She saw him turn around and give Karim some backchat receiving a backhand across the jaw for his trouble. Izzy gasped as the boy spun and fell to the ground.

"Bastard!" she said under her breath. "You'll pay for that." But that would have to wait.

She scanned the surroundings for Adam, but could not see him amongst the men there. They must have him hidden in one of the buildings.

Just then a crackling behind her alerted her to fact she was not alone. Just as she was turning to see who it was, Izzy felt large hands close around her throat. Her own hands automatically flew to them to try and prise them off. As she struggled, her assailant squeezed harder and her vision starting to blur. She had to act fast to escape this attack.

Mustering all her energy, Izzy stood and pushed her attacker's arms up and away. He fell back, and Izzy spun around to see him composing himself and rushing toward her. Summoning all her knowledge of hand-to-hand combat, Izzy got ready for battle. She bunched her hands into fists, waited until he was in range and swung at him catching him on the nose.

The man stumbled backwards, his hands flying to his face as blood spurted everywhere. Before he could regroup, Izzy sprang at him, knife out. Using her weight to knock him off his feet, as he fell backwards. She went with him, using her weapon to cut a deep slit across his throat. He gargled briefly and then was still.

Izzy clambered to her feet and wiped her knife on her trousers. She was covered from head to toe in blood. She could feet it starting to congeal on her face, but by that point, she didn't care. This was all the better for making her appear more terrifying to any other guard that got in her way.

Izzy went back to her hiding place and checked the yard again. Her fight with the guard had not attracted any attention, she saw with relief. Time to get going, she thought as she began to creep towards the house

While the men were distracted loading the van, Izzy snuck up to the farmhouse and peered into the first window. The room was in darkness and empty. It was the same for the next three windows, but at the fourth she found what she was looking for.

Adam, bloody and beaten, was tied to a chair in a dimly lit room. His eyes were swollen and closed, and he appeared to be unconscious. However, as she opened the window and crawled inside, he started and opened them. Recognition lit up his eyes, and he gave her a blood-tinged smile, then must have thought better of it.

"Jesus fuck! What happened to you?" he croaked, wincing with the effort of talking. A large purple bruise marred the flesh under one eye, and blood trickled down the side of his face.

Izzy frowned and then inspected herself. In her desire to free her lover, she had forgotten all about the bloody mess she was in. "Oh, none of it's mine," she said, going to him.

A sound from outside made both of them freeze. Adam's eyes widened with fright.

"Izzy, you've got to go," he hissed. "Get out of here before they capture you as well."

"I'm going nowhere." She unsheathed the knife and began to saw at his bonds.

"Please! I couldn't bear it if something happened to you because of me," he said, looking at her with imploring eyes.

"We really need to have a big talk when all this is over." Izzy cut through one rope.

"Please, Iz, save yourself. Go and get the police."

"Not without you, and definitely not without Aaron." She released his hands. "Don't worry, Adam, it's all good. Remember when I said I had new talents now?"

"Yes?" He rubbed his wrists.

She went to work on the rope binding his feet, severing it in no time. "Well, these are some of them."

144

Adam was quiet as he attempted to get to his feet. The beating he had taken had obviously affected his balance, for when he stood, he swayed wildly and was on the verge of collapse. Izzy caught him under the arm just as he was about to go down and helped him to stand. He gasped in pain as she put her arm around his back.

"What do you mean new talents?" he wheezed as he took a step. "Are you in the SAS or something?"

"Not quite." Izzy was about to talk some more when they heard the sound of heavy footsteps in the corridor outside the room. "Shhh," she warned as the footsteps moved off in the opposite direction and went quiet. "Okay, so we can't go out the usual way. We'll just have to leave the way I came in."

Izzy guided him towards the window and with each step, he seemed to be revived a little more.

"I need you to climb out of this window and find help."

He paused. "I'm not leaving you alone."

"I'm a big girl and can take care of myself."

"I'm not leaving you. Don't even ask me to." There was a real determination in his voice, and Izzy knew better than to argue. "I want to help."

"Alright, but you do exactly what I say, understood?" Izzy never had help on missions. It was too distracting, but she had no choice now.

He nodded.

"Follow me."

Izzy checked the coast was clear before helping Adam through the window. Once she was sure he wouldn't collapse on the other side, Izzy clambered out. With Adam unsteady at her back, she crept around the building, keeping herself low and in the shadows as much as possible. Then she brought them to a halt at the corner of the house and within sight of the yard.

"The only way this will work," she whispered to Adam as he crouched beside her, "is if we keep the element of surprise." She peered around the corner and quickly pulled back.

"There are five of them, all with guns, including Karim," she said. "Good odds." Izzy gave Adam a once-over. He was clearly still suffering from his injuries. "Are you sure you can do this?"

"I can," he replied in an instant. It felt good that he had her back. Wriggling out of the backpack, Izzy removed the flash-bangs and smoke bombs from the side pockets and handed them to Adam.

"How's your ball arm?"

Adam ignored the comment, studying the devices. "What am I to do with these?"

"It's all part of the plan," she began and then she told him exactly what she wanted him to do. Adam nodded as she took him through it all. They couldn't allow the men to leave the complex with the boys, and it was too dangerous to go in with guns blazing, so this was the best bet.

"Give me five minutes and then start throwing those," she said, nodding at the flashbangs and smoke bombs. Then she handed him a handgun. "Do you know how to use this?"

He looked at it and shook his head. She took the safety off and gave it back to him.

"Just point and squeeze the trigger," she said. "But only use it if you absolutely have to."

She patted his shoulder and stood up.

"Izzy?" Adam said.

She turned around.

"Don't die," he said. "I've kind of got used to being around you again."

"I won't, I promise." Izzy bent down and kissed him tenderly on his lips. "Don't worry, you're not getting rid of me that easily."

Leaving Adam in position and keeping the shadows as much as possible, she made her way along the outer edge of the courtyard, all the time getting closer to the enslaved boys. From her hiding point, Izzy watched the last one was climbing up. The bright green colour of his cap and pasty white skin told her instantly it was Aaron.

I'd better get a shift on, she thought, and took up position behind the staff sleeping quarters nearest the van. Any minute now all hell was going to break loose, and those bastards wouldn't know what hit them. Izzy placed a gas mask over her face, took the handgun out of the rucksack and waited.

Seconds later, the sounds of small explosions, flashes and loud bangs filled the air, and dense white smoke began to drift across the yard. From inside the van, the boys screamed as the guards were blinded by the smoke and began to shoot their guns indiscriminately.

Time to go.

Izzy ran around the building and made her way to the van. Breathing hard in the gas mask, she met with one guard who was running away from the smoke bombs, his rifle slung across his shoulders banging off his legs as he ran. In one swift action, she hit him smack across the jaw with the butt of her handgun, sending him flying into the smoke.

As he disappeared from sight, Izzy kept running and just made it to the back of the van as another man was closing the doors. With no hesitation, she raised her gun and shot him between the eyes. The force of the impact sent the man's body flying back, giving her free access to the van.

Wasting no more time, Izzy flew at the doors and yanked on the handle. It opened easily and Izzy threw open the doors just as more bangs were heard in the yard. In the back of the van, the boys cried out in fright and cowered as far away from her as possible. All except one. With a rebel yell, Aaron lunged forward, fists up ready to fight.

"Aaron, it's me!" she yelled through her mask. "It's Izzy!"

The young Glaswegian boy paused, put his fists down and grinned. Then he began to cough violently as the smoke seeped into the van.

Izzy motioned for him and the other boys to come to her. "This way! Quickly!" she yelled.

Aaron leapt out of the van and then turned to encourage the others. "Come on!" he shouted. "Come on!"

Needing no other reassurance, the boys rushed forward and streamed out of the vehicle. One by one, they congregated at Izzy until there were eleven frightened children standing before her, far more than she had first thought. It didn't matter. She would ensure they would all escape. She turned to Aaron.

"Get them into the safety of the farmhouse, and I'll come and get you once I've dealt with this lot," she said. He nodded and began to lead the boys towards the building.

Izzy turned back and was immediately sent flying. Karim! The tall African grinned as she hit the deck, her head buzzing with pain. Shaking it off, Izzy scrambled to her feet just as her assailant sent her spinning again with an uppercut to the jaw. The force of the punch dislodged the gas mask and cracked the eye lenses.

Damnit, Izzy, get a grip, she scolded herself as she yanked the mask off and threw it aside.

Blood, her own this time, trickled down her face and she

tasted the distinct metal taste on her lips. Izzy stood up again and swung the handgun up to fire, but too late, Karim had already anticipated her move and smacked it from her hand. The gun went flying off to the side and was lost in the smoke.

Fuck!

The big African, a mad look in his eyes, stomped towards her. Izzy frantically looked around for a weapon of some sort and her eyes rested on the guard at the van. She ran over, pulled his gun from the waist holster and trained it on Karim. Bam! Bam! Two shots hit her assailant square between his eyes. The big man looked startled at first and then his eyes rolled in his head as he dropped down dead at her feet. Izzy sighed with relief and went to his body. She gave it a vicious kick in the groin.

"That's for hitting my boy." She kicked the body again. "And that's for Adam."

"What's for Adam?" a voice said behind her.

Izzy turned to see the tall Scot standing before her, still holding a gun. Relief washed over her that he was okay, despite the beating he had taken earlier. She rushed over to him and kissed him passionately on the lips, causing him to wince and pull away with pain.

"Easy," he said. "The old lips are a bit sore still." Then he stared down at Karim, lying on the dusty ground, eyes bulging.

"Is he dead?"

"Yes," she replied, sticking the gun into the small of her back and taking her mobile from her trouser pocket. "Did you see where the other two guards disappeared to?"

"They got into a car and drove off."

"Good." She opened the phone and dialled.

"Who are you calling? The police?"

"Something like that."

She held up a finger indicating the call had been answered.

"Wrath, it's Envy," she began. "Yes, the boys are secure... Yeah, everything's fine, but we need to be evacuated... and there are more of them than we first thought...eleven in total, plus me and Adam..."

"And them too," said Adam pointing at the adult workers who were now emerging from their living quarters.

Izzy frowned. "Scrub that," she said, "it's actually around 30 people in total...I know I said that but...What?... I ... Okay... Ok-ay... that's great... just see what you can do."

She closed down the call and turned her attention to Adam. "She's sending us some transport," she said.

He nodded. Then her attention was caught by the guard she had felled earlier. He was reaching in the dusty earth for her dropped handgun.

"Shit!"

Izzy took up her gun, aimed and shot him square in the chest. The guard fell backwards, blood oozing from the wound, dead as dead can be. Izzy refocussed on Adam's horrified face. She shrugged.

"We can't afford to have witnesses," she explained. "Besides, he was reaching for a gun."

"What now?"

"Now we wait."

As they turned intending to wait inside the farmhouse, their way was blocked by the adult workers. They were walking slowly towards them, a mixture of fear and wonder on their faces. The oldest man approached Adam and took his hand. He shook it and grinned showing off a set of perfectly white teeth.

"You rescued us?" he said in broken English. "You hero."

"Well, it wasn't actually me..." Adam started to say. He

looked at Izzy who was standing nearby, amusement on her face. "It was…" But before he could say anything, the older man turned to his colleagues.

"This man saved us," the worker shouted in French. "He is our hero."

The other men began to surround Adam, and each one insisted on shaking his hand and patting him on the back. Adam's protestations that he was not the hero fell on deaf ears, and he gave Izzy a desperate look, mouthing 'help me' as he became surrounded. She shook her head and just grinned, briefly enjoying the moment. Then she started to move towards the house again.

Izzy shoved her handgun into the back of her belt and took stock as she walked. Wrath was sending some sort of transport for the boys and the workers, but that wouldn't be arriving for a while. In the meantime, the boys would need to be reassured that they weren't going from one terrible regime to another. She reached the porch and climbed the steps, wrapped up in her plans.

They'll need fed and a change of clothes, she thought. Her head was a swirl of plans and ideas of how to get the boys back to their families. For now, she mused as she walked along the wooden porch, the first thing they'll need is to know they were safe.

Chapter 18 - Estelle

The building was in darkness, save for the porch lights and a light in the windows of the living room. Knowing all the guards to be dead, Izzy was less cautious about entering the house. Humming quietly, she moved down the quiet hallway and made her way towards the living room at the end.

Izzy was coming down from the high of the rescue and was enjoying the feeling that she had saved the boys from further slavery or, worse, an horrific death. Her footsteps echoed along the wooden floor and she resisted the urge to skip. It had been a good day's work; the boys were safe and so was Adam. It wasn't over yet. She still had to get the boys to safety, but they were so close. She couldn't wait to tell them they were going home.

The living room door was shut when she approached, and she opened it with a happy grin on her face.

"It's just me, Aaron," she called as she pushed it open.

The door swung away from her, creaking as it went, and revealed a group of terrified looking boys all bunched together on a sofa and chairs in one corner of the room. No one spoke as she paused at the doorway and had a good look around her. There was no need for them to be so scared, she thought, they were free.

Cautiously, Izzy took a step inside, then another and then heard a click and felt something cold and metal being pushed into the back of her head. A gun. She had no doubt about that. Shit! Someone had been hiding behind the door and had caught her. She had been so full of joy that the boys had been rescued that she had never thought to look. What a rookie mistake. Silently, she cursed her own stupidity.

"Well, well, well," said a familiar voice with a French accent. Izzy caught a waft of expensive perfume. "So, you're still meddling in my business?"

"Estelle."

Suddenly it all made sense: how Karim and his crew knew that they were coming on a fact-finding visit, who put Koffi in their room and who tipped the plantation guards off to remove the boys from the site. Izzy was furious with herself for not realising sooner that it was Estelle who was behind it all.

"And here was me thinking we were such good friends." Izzy began to slowly turn around so that she might look her attacker in the eye, but received a knock on the temple for her troubles.

"Uh-huh," Estelle warned. "'Ands up, that's right."

Izzy felt her former classmate remove her gun from its position on the small of her back and then shove her from behind. She stumbled forward.

"Be a good girl and go and sit down beside the boys," Estelle ordered.

Izzy glanced back at her and saw the French woman was holding a Smith & Wesson Magnum at head height. "That's a hefty piece to be carrying around with you," she said as she slowly walked towards the boys.

"What's it to you which 'andgun I 'ave?" Estelle snapped.

Izzy shrugged. "I was just saying, that's all."

"Yet another thing of mine that is none of your business," she retorted. "Sit down."

Izzy sat on an armchair near Aaron. The teen was looking at her with real fear in his eyes, and she wished she could have given him a hug and tell him everything was going to be okay.

"You just couldn't leave it alone, could you?" Estelle continued as she walked further into the room. "You just had to keep meddling. I thought leaving the boy in your bed would send you a message, but you chose to ignore it. You just 'ad to be the big hero and come and save them, didn't you? Well, you're not so big now, are you, Isabella?" Estelle spat out Izzy's name like it was poison.

Izzy turned in the chair to face her foe. "You took friends of mine. Of course I was going to come and get them."

Estelle snarled. "You had no right."

"And you had no right to enslave these boys," Izzy growled. "It was you, wasn't it, Estelle, or did Daddy have the idea for this form of cheap labour?"

"My father is straight up goody-two shoes when it comes to labour laws. 'E'd never put a foot out of place or cut corners to get real results. But Lorenz was failing, costs were too 'igh and something needed to be done to get the company back on an even keel." Estelle walked to the centre of the room. "I volunteered to manage the change, and my father was delighted when I improved the 'arvest whilst getting costs down. 'E never knew I was using these boys." There was pride in her voice. "And 'e was so proud of me."

"And how did you get the boys to work here? Put an ad in the local paper?"

"Ah, that's where darling Karim came in. It was 'is job to procure the workers. Young boys are so much easier to steal than fully grown men, so 'e would go across the border and just take them. Sometimes, it was as easy as asking their families to sell them, but mostly 'e just took them. Of course, they don't tend to last longer than a year, but there was always plenty more."

She caressed the face of the boy sitting nearest to her. He flinched and tried to pull away, but she grabbed his face and squeezed until he yelped. "That's the good thing about these Africans. They 'ave plenty of children."

Izzy scowled. "I always thought you were a bit of a bitch at uni, but now I know you're the Queen of the Bitches."

"Well, 'ow is it you Brits say it…if the shoe fits?" Estelle smiled.

"Let them go, Estelle," Izzy said. "It's over. Your men are dead, and the police are on their way."

"It's only over when I say it's over," Estelle snapped. "Who would 'ave thought it would 'ave been you who brought my whole operation down? Little old Isabella Starr."

She walked towards the window and looked out.

"What I can't understand is why you did it," Izzy said. She mouthed to Aaron, 'throw your voice'. He looked puzzled and mouthed back 'what?'. "You could have just hired men and paid them properly," Izzy continued. "Why enslave boys with all the risks that comes with? I thought you were smarter than that."

She pointed to Aaron and mimed 'throw your voice'. At first, he did not seem to get what she was asking him to do, but on her repeating the mime, he nodded.

"Because we can pay them less, because they are more pliable…" Estelle said as she turned back around. She frowned at Izzy.

"But they are children," Izzy said.

"And? Children 'ave been working for centuries." Estelle scoffed.

"It's not right. They should be in school. They should be enjoying their childhood, not holed up on some cocoa farm working long hours for you," Izzy said. Then a thought occurred to her. "Where are these children from? How did they get here?"

"Why do you want to know that? What does it matter?"

"Koffi's note said he and his friends were from Burkina Faso. How did a boy so young travel from there to the Ivory Coast?"

Estelle shrugged. "I did what I 'ad to do to prove to my father I could make our farms profitable." she said.

"You mean this is happening on other farms?" Izzy couldn't stop the horror from entering her voice. "How many?"

"What difference does it make?" Estelle sneered.

Just then a Scotsman's voice was heard out in the hallway.

"Stop!! It's the police!" Aaron was throwing his voice again.

Estelle startled and glanced over to the door. As she did this, Izzy leapt from her chair and grabbed Estelle's hand that was holding the gun. As the women wrestled for the weapon, the boys squealed, and Aaron tried his best to help. He stuck his foot out in an attempt to trip up Estelle, but it was Izzy who took the tumble and ended up face first on the floor, giving her head a hefty bang as she went down.

"Fuck!" she heard Aaron yell as she slowly came back to her senses. Izzy tried to sit up then heard the gun safety catch click.

"I wouldn't if I were you," said Estelle, pointing the large handgun at her. Izzy lay down again.

She grabbed a hold of Aaron and held the gun to his head. Pulling him, she made him walk with her to the door.

"Goodbye, Isabella," she said. "I would like to say it was nice seeing you again, but I'd be lying." She smiled. "Oh, and don't think of trying to follow me or stop me," she said, "or this boy of yours will be killed. Do you understand?"

Izzy watched helplessly as Estelle disappeared out of the room, a terrified Aaron at her side. Shit!

As soon as they were gone, Izzy was back on her feet and running to the doorway. She looked around the room and found her gun on a table near the door. Estelle must have put it there when she disarmed her. She picked it up and ran after them.

Out in the dark corridor she paused to ascertain which way Estelle and Aaron had gone. Although the living room was at one end of the house, at the bottom of a long corridor, there were many rooms off to each side. Estelle could have chosen any one of these by which to leave the building, but she hadn't.

In the gloom, Izzy could see the French woman drag Aaron down to the other end and enter a door there. Losing no more time, she raced after them, determined to rescue Aaron and to ensure her former classmate did not escape justice. Running hard, Izzy reached the doorway in record time and carefully pushed it open.

She was in the kitchen. A large modern space, the stainless worktops and utensils shone dimly in the light of under-cabinet spotlights. The kitchen was empty, but a back door hung open, so it was to there she ran. Remembering her training, she cautiously peeked around the doorjamb just in time to see Izzy force Aaron into a brand-new Mercedes Benz SUV. The French woman then climbed into the driver's seat and started the car up. The engine roared into life, and the car took off just as Izzy ran outside and raised her handgun. Too late, she let off a couple of rounds, aiming at the tyres in an attempt to stop Estelle getting away.

"Damnit!"

There were no more vehicles at the rear of the building, but Izzy knew there were some at the front. Now feeling exhausted from the events of the day, she mustered the last ounce of energy she had left in her body and ran around to the front of the farmhouse. Adam was still there talking to the farmhands. His worried expression met hers.

"Izzy?" he shouted as she raced to a nearby jeep and leapt in. "What's going on? Where are you going?"

"She's getting away!"

Izzy felt for the keys in the ignition, but there were none. Shit. She thought for a moment, her head buzzing with fear that Estelle would harm Aaron. Then she noticed that the jeep was not modern—it was an old one and that made her smile. Older vehicles did not have the same anti-theft safeguards the new ones had and that would work to her advantage. Fumbling underneath the steering column, Izzy pulled a couple of wires down. Taking two, she pressed them together and the car growled into life.

You might be old, she thought as she let the handbrake off and put her foot on the accelerator, but there's still loads in you yet.

"Izzy, wait! I'll come with you!" Adam shouted as she whizzed past.

"No time!" And with that, she was gone.

Izzy was a few minutes behind Estelle, but could see the SUV up ahead on the road out of the plantation. The car did not slow down at the gate, but headed straight through and on to the main road. It turned left. Putting her foot down, Izzy followed, also taking a left turn when she reached the gates.

Although the SUV was brand spanking new, Izzy hoped that

it would not handle the poor Ivory Coast roads as well as she knew the jeep would. The potholes would surely slow Estelle down, she prayed. But it was not to be, not only did Estelle's vehicle handle the terrain well, but it seemed to be getting away from her.

Izzy knew then she had two options: continue trying to catch up and apprehend Estelle or follow at a distance and pounce later. She chose the latter and allowed the jeep to fall back a bit. She could still see the SUV's headlights in the distance and that gave her hope that she wouldn't be too late. She had no idea where Estelle was headed, but she knew that once she got there, Aaron would be of no further use to her. The teenager would be killed.

That's what I'd do if I was in Estelle's position, Izzy thought glumly. Hold on! Where are they going?

Some distance away, the SUV was turning off to the right and heading into the bush. Izzy could still make its headlights out as it rumbled along what she assumed was another dirt track. Putting her foot down again, she raced to the turn off and followed as closely as she dared.

****

In the SUV, Aaron sat with his eyes closed and his seatbelt firmly clipped in. Estelle was driving like a crazy woman, and every time he tried to speak, she stuck her Magnum in his face and told him to shut up. He peeked at his captor and wished he hadn't. Estelle had a manic look on her face, like a lion cornered by hunters. There was no way she was going to go down without a fight, and he knew that. He hoped and prayed that Izzy would somehow come and rescue him, because he knew if she didn't, his days were numbered. He would not come out of this alive.

"Nearly there!" He heard Estelle say with a strange glee.

Aaron opened his eyes and found himself in a large illuminated clearing in the jungle. In the middle of the clearing was a round concrete platform on which the letter 'H' had been painted. Estelle drove the car into the clearing and parked. Then she turned to Aaron and held the gun up.

"Out of the car!" she growled.

"But..."

"Now!" She pushed the gun towards him, and he didn't argue.

Aaron undid his seatbelt and fumbled for the door handle. Gripping it tightly, he opened the door and slid out. Briefly, he had the idea of making a run for it into the bush, but quickly discarded that when he remembered that this was Africa, at night, and there were big scary beasts in the jungle. Besides, he told himself as he gingerly made his way around the car towards Estelle, he was sure she would have no hesitation in shooting him in the back. She pointed the gun at him again and made him put his hands up.

Keeping her gun trained on Aaron, Estelle removed her cell phone from her pocket and dialled.

"How long now?" she said into it. "Yes, I'm 'ere already... five minutes?... Good." She hung up and turned her attention on the boy. "So," she said, "what are we going to do with you, now I don't need you anymore?"

"You could let me go?" he said. "I won't tell. Promise."

"If only it were that easy," she smirked. "No, I think the best plan is to dispose of you. A quick shot through the 'ead will do the trick." Her face was a mask of pure evil, and Aaron could see she was enjoying this.

"No!" he squealed. "You don't have to do that!" He began to

back away. "You don't have to kill me. I'm not a threat to you!"

"Yes, but you're important to Izzy, and killing you would make her upset, which would make me happy."

Aaron desperately looked around for an escape or a weapon, but could see no way out of it. He stood there, heart racing, wondering what to do next, when the distant sound of a helicopter could be heard above.

Estelle looked up at the starlit sky and smiled. "Ah, that's my lift."

And that's my cue, Aaron thought as he made a bolt for it.

Keeping his head low, he ran away from Estelle and into the scary dark of the jungle. He was terrified of lions and tigers, but he would rather take his chances with them than stand and allow a mad woman to shoot him. He scrambled blindly in the darkness, falling on roots and over boulders, cutting his knees, scraping his hands and arms, but he didn't care. Fear and adrenaline were coursing through him. He was not intending to die today.

*****

As Aaron was making his escape, Izzy's jeep had reached the end of the road and emerged into the clearing. The sound of the engine caught Estelle's attention and she trained her gun on it. Bam! Bam! Two rounds were fired catching the Jeep in the windscreen, shattering the glass, and causing Izzy to swerve and crash into the SUV. Battered and bruised, the assassin quickly pulled herself together, grabbed her gun and jumped out of the damaged vehicle before Estelle could finish her off.

"Come out, come out, wherever you are!" Estelle called as she searched for Izzy.

Keeping low behind the two cars, Izzy carefully made her

way around and peeked around the bonnet of the SUV. Estelle, obviously not aware of where Izzy was, was walking in the opposite direction. Above them, a large helicopter with the Lorenz logo was beginning its descent towards them, it's downdraft whipping up the dry dust of the ground all around them.

"Give it up, Estelle, you know you've got nowhere to run," Izzy called, hoping her former friend would come quietly.

"That's where you're wrong, Izzy," Estelle replied. "I've got loads of places I can go. In fact, 'ere's my way out now."

In the dust storm created by the helicopter, Izzy squinted to see the helicopter land on the 'H' in the centre of the platform. The blades were still turning, but that didn't stop Estelle from taking her chances and running towards it. Izzy could see that if she ran after her, she wouldn't be able to catch Estelle. There was only one thing to do. It would be difficult, but she thought she could pull it off.

Leaning on the bonnet of the SUV, Izzy steadied her gun. Taking a deep breath, she squeezed the trigger, and a round shot from the barrel and hurtled towards Estelle. The French woman, thinking herself safe, had now discarded her own piece and was running towards the open door of the helicopter like her life depended on it. The noise of the helicopter engines was terrible and masked the sounds of the gunfire.

As Izzy watched, one bullet caught Estelle on the shoulder, made her spin and then drop to the ground. She lay there, clutching her arm and squealing in rage. Now Izzy leapt into action. She ran at her foe, put her foot on her chest to keep her down and pointed her gun at her.

"By rights, I should kill you right here and now," Izzy said. "But it's your lucky day. I'm going to let the police deal with you instead." She glared at her fallen enemy. "Have you ever been inside an Ivory Coast jail, Estelle? I hear they are just peachy."

"What are you talking about?" Estelle gasped. She looked back at the helicopter. "My people, 'ere, won't let you do that."

Izzy smirked. "I don't think so." She nodded, indicating Estelle should look at the helicopter and the fallen French woman gasped when she saw who was inside. Inspector Sita N'Zi stepped out along with two uniformed officers. Two others, hidden by the dark interior of the helicopter, could be seen in the background.

"No, you can't do this," Estelle said, eyes wide with fear. "You can't do this! Don't you people know who I am? Wait until my father 'ears about this!" Then seeing her words held no track, she changed her tack. "Look, I can pay you," she continued. "Whatever you want. Just let me go and I'll make sure you are well compensated." She looked at Sita. "You could use some extra cash, couldn't you?"

"Madamoiselle Estelle Allard, I am arresting you on suspicion of the murder of Koffi and for the trafficking end enslavement of boys and men." Sita nodded and the two officers helped the bleeding Estelle to her feet. As one fastened a pair of metal handcuffs on to Estelle's good arm and attached it to his own, Estelle yelled, "Why are you arresting me? It should be her who's going to jail. She murdered all of my men."

Sita turned her attention to Izzy. "Is this true?"

Izzy shrugged. "They were the ones who attacked me," she said. "I was defending myself."

Sita looked dubious, but dismissed the explanation. "No matter," she said. "We will find out the truth in due course. Meanwhile, I'd like to thank you, Madamoiselle Starr, for helping us apprehend this woman. We greatly appreciate it."

Izzy, unused to praise, could merely stand awkwardly. Should she thank her? Should she say nothing? What does a person do in this type of situation? Then she suddenly remembered something. Aaron! Where was Aaron?

"Thank you," she replied, "but if you'll excuse me, I have someone I must find."

She turned to Estelle. "What did you do with Aaron?" she hissed.

Estelle smirked at her. "I shot him in the face and shoved his bloody body out of the car!" she lied and laughed heartily.

It was all Izzy could do to stop herself from launching at Estelle and tearing the bitch's eyes out. Just then, she heard a familiar voice shout her name. Aaron emerged from the bush covered in scratches, but otherwise unharmed. She ran towards him.

"I'm so glad you are safe," she said, giving him a hug.

It was at that moment that Izzy realised that there was a man with a very familiar face had disembarked the helicopter and was striding towards her. Biko was grinning and looking very pleased with himself.

"Ah, Miss Envy. I'm so very pleased you are unharmed," he said. "Now before we go any further, may I introduce you to someone?" He turned to the helicopter and beckoned to someone inside. A tall striking woman got out and walked towards them.

"Miss Envy, this is Moussa Kambou," he said. "She's the Minister of the Interior and Security. She has long been fighting against child slavery and people trafficking in this part of the world."

Izzy stepped forward and offered her hand. "Hello, it's an honour to meet you."

"Likewise," Moussa replied, shaking her hand. "I must

thank you, Miss Envy, for all that you have done here. You have stopped some very nasty people from abusing children. I know very little of your organisation, but Biko here described you as the good guys. I hope that is correct."

Izzy smiled. "Yes, you could say that," she said and crossed her fingers behind her back.

"But it is a secret organisation and your presence here should not be known to all and sundry? Is that correct?" the Minister asked. Izzy nodded. "It is such a pity, for I would have loved to publicly acknowledge how you saved those boys from slavery and certain death. However, I know that cannot be."

"It's alright, ma'am," Izzy replied. "Knowing they are now safe is good enough for us."

"And where are these children?"

"Back at the plantation, inside the farmhouse. I thought it better they remain there until help could arrive," Izzy replied.

"Well," replied Moussa, "help has arrived."

While the police officers took Estelle back to headquarters in her own car, Izzy, Aaron and Moussa drove back to the plantation in the beaten-up old jeep. Izzy briefly felt embarrassed that someone of Moussa's standing in the community should have to be seen in such a dilapidated old banger, but Moussa seemed perfectly happy sitting in the passenger seat.

"Don't worry, Miss Envy," she said as the car turned up the drive leading to the farmhouse, "I will make sure the boys are taken care of and sent back to their homeland."

She had spoken to Wrath, she said, and together they had made arrangements to get them to a place of safety and then back home, if that was what the boys wanted. As they drew up to the courtyard, Moussa asked about Estelle.

"Her father is the SEO of the company that owns this property, is that right?" she enquired.

"He is, but he doesn't seem to have been any part of the enslaving of these people," Izzy said. "Estelle told me he was totally in the dark about it all."

Moussa nodded. "We'll look into him anyway."

Adam was in the farmhouse kitchen organising two of the men to make food for everyone when Izzy, Aaron and Moussa entered the building. It had been a hard night, and they were all, men and boys, showing signs of exhaustion.

"I thought a quick meal of something would make everyone feel better," he explained after Izzy introduced him to the minister.

"Excuse me a moment." Adam leaned in and gave Izzy a chaste kiss on the lips. "I'm so happy you're okay," he murmured. "I was so worried. You just took off."

"I'm good," she replied. "And I told you: I can take care of myself."

"Yes, but…"

"Yes, but nothing," she said with a giggle. "Now, where is everyone? I want to introduce them to Moussa."

The boys and the rest of the plantation's cocoa workers were all sitting in the living room awaiting rescue. They perked up when the two women and Aaron entered the room. After a short introduction from Izzy, Moussa took them through their plans to get them to safety.

"For now, though, rest," she added. She turned to the assassin. "Miss Envy," she began. The African woman pulled her in for a tight hug. Startled at first, Izzy hugged her back. "How can I tell you how grateful we are for what you and your friends have done? On behalf of the Ivory Coast, I would like to give you my sincere thanks. Now, what can we do for you?"

Izzy thought for a moment and then bit her lip.

"Funny you should say that…!" she began.

An hour later, dried blood tightening her skin, Izzy found herself seated in the helicopter with Adam and Aaron at her side. It was the first time either Adam or Aaron had been in one and, despite their tiredness, both were relaxed and excited. Under cover of darkness, they were being taken out of the country to a small private airstrip on the border with Ghana.

The helicopter flight took only half an hour. In the deep darkness of the night, Izzy was disappointed that she couldn't see more of the country, but that was just part of the job. The sun was beginning to rise by the time the helicopter had landed and they had boarded a small private jet sent by Wrath. She knew it was from her sister, for as soon as they had buckled themselves into the soft leather seats, the stewardess came round with a tray of coffee and some American donuts.

"Compliments of the management," the stewardess said as she offered the plate to Izzy. Izzy took one and bit into it. It was delicious and sugary, and exactly what she needed. "I also have a message for you, Miss Envy, but I'm not sure whether I should give it to you or not."

"Oh? Who from?"

"It's from someone calling herself Wrath. I'm sorry about this, but she told me I had to tell you this or she would cause trouble. She said I was to say don't eat too many donuts, there's nothing worse than a fugly sister." The stewardess looked at Izzy in fear.

"She said that, did she?" Izzy smiled and then a great big chuckle erupted. Trust Wrath to be so cheeky!

Chapter 19 - Creedie

The farm was a welcome sight after the last few days, and Izzy asked Adam to stay. They needed to work out what it was between them: an on-job fling or something deep and meaningful. She wasn't sure she could totally trust him with her heart again, but was willing to hear what he had to say.

They arrived to Dinghy and Robert standing at the kitchen door and Bob, tongue out, racing up to car as it came up the hill. Mary had insisted on meeting them with the four-wheel drive at the airport when they had arrived two hours earlier. Rolling her eyes at Izzy's blood-stained clothing, she never-the-less didn't put her off giving her a hug. She shook hands with Adam and glared at Aaron for daring to defy her. All the way back, she scolded him for disappearing on them and flying out to Africa. The teenager, for his part, apologised several times, promising never to do it again.

"You're right you won't," Mary said as she drove the car up the dirt track leading to the farmhouse. "I'm confiscating your passport."

"You can't do that," the teen replied from the back seat. "What if I want to go on holiday?"

"Holiday? There will be no holidays until I'm convinced you're mature enough to go on holiday," she snapped. She turned to Izzy. "I'm so relieved you are all safe. I was really worried this time. We all thought you were goners."

The car pulled up outside the farmhouse.

"You know I'm always careful, Mary." Izzy's voice was reassuring.

"Yeah, but you had Aaron in tow. I just had a bad feeling about this one and Dinghy even started planning your funeral," Mary confessed. She winked at Aaron as she switched the engine off. Izzy and Adam suppressed their laughter.

"What?"

"Yeah, Robert even phoned the priest in Helensburgh to see if he would do a memorial service," Robert added.

"Why would you do that?" Aaron followed Izzy out of the car. "I'm not even Catholic!"

As the Aaron and Mary continued their conversation into the house, Adam took Izzy's hand and looked deeply into her eyes.

"I thought you were a goner too," he confessed.

"There's no way anyone's going to kill me." Izzy flipped her hair. "I'm practically super human!" she joked.

He pulled her towards him and put his arm around her shoulder. They both looked at the view. From the farm, they had a spectacular view of Loch Lomond and the surrounding mountains. To the left was the cloud-covered peak of Ben Lomond and below, glittering in the weak winter sunlight, the long expanse of the loch spread out before them.

"Stunning," he said.

"It is," she agreed.

"I wasn't talking about the view." He grinned, gazing down

at her. She rolled her eyes at the cheesy compliment, but couldn't help but smile.

"You know, I could kiss you right now," he said in a low voice.

She looked up at him. "Well, what's stopping you?"

"About five pints of someone else's blood," he confessed, inspecting her stained shirt.

"Ah yes," Izzy said, pulling away from him. "I'd forgotten about that. Come on. Let's get cleaned up."

****

A quick reviving shower, a change of clothes and Izzy joined Adam and the rest of them in her kitchen to eat some takeaway pizza Dinghy had ordered for them all. As they sat around the kitchen table, Izzy, Aaron and Adam related their African adventures to an appreciative audience.

"And then Izzy went down and the French woman grabbed me and dragged me outside," Aaron said, eyes wide with the excitement of telling the story. "I thought I was a goner, but then Izzy appeared and next thing I knew Izzy shot her, and Estelle fell to the ground and that was her." He took another bite of pizza. "Of course, I knew Izzy wouldn't let her take me. I'm too precious." He gave them all a grin.

"Aye, precious in the head!" Dinghy gave the boy a playful shove.

"Then we got this private jet home. It was amazing. All mod cons and great food," the boy said enthusiastically. "It even had seats that turned in to beds. We were able to sleep all the way home. It was brilliant."

"Well," Mary said, "I'm glad you're all back safe and

sound."She gave Izzy a look.

"I know," Izzy said, "but it's the nature of the job."

"Talking of which," Adam said interrupting, "you never really did explain to me exactly what you do for a living."

Izzy looked around her friends gathered there at the table. Those in the know nodded in agreement. Their eyes said it all: it would be okay to tell him.

"I… I…" Izzy wasn't sure how Adam was going to take this. "I kind of…um…"

"Yes?" he said.

"I sort of…" Oh shit, this was going to ruin everything. How could she tell the man she loved she killed people for a living? Shit! Did I just say 'man I loved'? "I… um…"

Just then there was the sound of a noisy car engine in the farm courtyard. It was as if someone was deliberately revving the engine to get their attention. Izzy looked in alarm at Mary who was equally looking uneasy.

"Were we expecting anyone, Mary?" Izzy got to her feet and walked to the kitchen window. She stayed hidden behind the open curtain and peeked out.

A large grey Mercedes Benz was sitting in their courtyard and three menacing men got out. One, who was obviously the boss, nodded to an underling who returned the nod and began to lumber towards the farmhouse. The whole scene smelled of trouble.

"Aaron, go upstairs," Izzy ordered as calmly as she could. "You too, Adam. Robert, Dinghy, Mary, get the firearms."

The team leapt into action immediately. They were well practised; Izzy had seen to that. Although she kept her home a secret from most people, she made sure she and her lodgers knew what to do if they were attacked. Because of her job, she always believed it would happen, and now it had. The three rushed out of the kitchen into the interior of the farmhouse as Adam and Aaron looked at Izzy in bewilderment.

"Upstairs! Now!" she hissed. Do not argue with me, the expression on her face said.

It was Aaron who moved first. He grabbed Adam by the arm and pulled him towards the hallway just as there was a loud rap of the front door. Izzy ushered the man and boy up the stairs and then went back into the kitchen to retrieve her handgun from the dresser drawer. Checking there were bullets in the barrel, she went to open the door.

Jamming one foot against the steel reinforced door, she opened it just wide enough to see who was knocking.

"Can I help you?" she asked the thug standing there. He was a big guy, well over six foot tall, with a scar on his cheeks and a muscular frame that screamed body builder. There was a plaster over his nose. It was the guy she had felled outside Bob Fleming's house. Shit.

"The boss wants to speak with you," he growled. His eyes flickered as if he recognised her, but he said nothing.

"Who's the boss?"

The thug turned and pointed. "That man over there."

She paused for a moment, thinking of all the things that could happen if she were to leave the safety of the building and go outside. Would the thug really try and take her again? Let him try.

"Okay, tell him to come forward and I'll speak to him, but only him. You and your friend over there…" She motioned with her head towards the second brute. "…need to stay next to the car, okay?"

"Okay."

He returned to his boss and related what she had just said. The man nodded and then walked forward. She tucked her gun into the small of her back and opened the door wider. As she did this, Mary, Dinghy and Robert reappeared each holding rifles.

"Take up your positions," she said, "and wait for my signal. I'll just be a minute. I don't know who these guys are or what they want, but they look like the mean business."

"Be careful," Mary said.

"Aren't I always?" Izzy replied with a rueful grin.

As she stepped outside, the wind whipped her hair and she felt a few raindrops hit her face. She tucked a stray strand of hair behind her ears and walked towards the man who apparently was the boss. He stopped halfway across the courtyard and waited until she had joined him before talking. He was a short, stocky, older man, with a gold tooth and dark, recently dyed hair that was gelled back across his head. He wore multiple rings on both hands and his clothes, a grey suit and white shirt, were expensive.

"Apologies for dropping in unannounced," he said with a heavy London accent, "but I've only just arrived in Scotland."

"Who are you and what do you want?"

"My name is Michael Creedie, and you have something of mine," he replied.

"I can assure you, Mr Creedie, I have nothing of yours," she replied. What the fuck?

"Let's not play silly beggars, Miss...um... what was your name?"

"You don't need my name," she rasped.

"Whatever. Anyway, give me what's mine, and we'll leave you good folks in peace." Creedie gave her a look that said if she didn't comply, there was going to be trouble. She laughed.

"I have no idea what you are talking about," she said. "Now get off my property before I make you get off my property."

"Now, let's be civil," he said. "I can assure you my item is indeed here. I know he is. We tracked his phone."

Ding ding ding ding. Realisation hit. Shit! He was talking about Aaron. I'm so stupid, thought Izzy, I should have checked he'd gotten rid of his cell phone. She felt panic rise in her gut, but she made sure she didn't show it on her face.

"His phone?"

"Yes, my boy, Aaron." A smug smile graced Creedie's face.

"He is here, isn't he?"

Izzy shrugged. "I don't know who you mean."

"Well, that's strange 'cos I can see him at the bedroom window up there right now," he replied, pointing at the farmhouse.

Izzy turned around just in time to see someone jump behind a curtain. Damnit!

"Now, let's be nice about this. I'll give you ten minutes to get the boy out here. He's mine, I own him and I'm taking him back to London."

"What if I don't? What if he doesn't want to go?" Izzy asked.

It was Creedie's turn to laugh. "You tell him, he owes me, and if he doesn't come, then his new friends are going to get hurt."

Izzy's eyes narrowed. "I can assure you I won't let that happen," she said in a low voice that was almost a growl.

"And how is a pretty girl like you going to stop me?"

She took a step forward. "You really don't want to find out the answer to that question, now do you Mr Creedie? My advice to you is to leave while you still can. Got it?"

Creedie's eyes narrowed. "I tell you what, girly," he began. "I'll give you half an hour to drag that brat out of the house or else we're going to come in there all guns blazing and get him ourselves."

"I'd like to see you try!" she growled.

"You have half an hour!" The thug returned to stand at his car leaving Izzy alone outside the house.

Fuck. Just when she thought they were all home safely, she had this to deal with.

Chapter 20 - Loch Lomond

Izzy returned to the farmhouse to find a terrified Aaron trembling behind the kitchen door. He had seen his former pimp from the upstairs window and had rushed down to see what was happening.

"What's going on?" he asked, breathless and red-faced from rushing down the stairs. "What are they doing here? How did they know I was here? Did they follow us from London?"

"Calm down, Aaron," Izzy said. "They tracked your phone, and they want you back."

"No!" He backed away. "I can't go back. I can't! Please don't make me!"

"That's not going to happen, I promise." Izzy put a hand on his arm. "I won't let them take you."

"But they'll hurt you," the scared boy said. "They'll hurt us all."

"No, they won't," Izzy said, rubbing his back. "Trust me on this."

"So, what are we going to do?" Adam had followed Aaron downstairs and was shocked to see Mary, Dinghy and Robert armed to the teeth in the kitchen.

"They've given us half an hour to get Aaron ready," Izzy replied, "so that should give us enough time to formulate a plan."

She gathered the troops around the table, and they quickly discussed what should happen next. Dinghy wanted to take them out using their shotguns, but Izzy soon dismissed that idea. She had had enough of death and didn't want to put any of her team at risk.

"No, I have a better idea." The people seated around the table leaned forward. "Here's what I think we should do…"

****

Izzy always kept a vehicle parked in a small barn attached to the farmhouse for emergencies. The Audi R8 was kept with a full tank of petrol and in perfect order to allow for a fast getaway should they need it. After confiscating Aaron's cell phone, Izzy led Adam, wearing Aaron's distinctive lime green baseball cap, into the barn via a door in the kitchen. They climbed into the car, and she started the engine.

The car roared into life and Izzy pressed a button on the car's dashboard which caused the automatic barn doors to swing open. Putting her foot down, the Audi shot out of the barn and screeched around the corner. As they went around to the front of the farmhouse, she could see Aaron's pimp and his henchmen start in surprise at the speed of the Audi as it moved towards them. As the Audi whizzed passed them, Michael Creedie and his men leapt out of the way, then scrambled into their own vehicle to pursue them.

The plan is working, she thought as Audi sped down the track. *They think Adam is Aaron. Good.*

"Now let's see how you handle the winding Highland roads," she said aloud.

The plan was simple: Izzy and Adam would lead them away

from the farmhouse whilst Mary, Robert and Dinghy bundled Aaron into the 4X4 and take him to a safe house in Stirling. They would all regroup there when Izzy had lost Aaron's tormentors.

The Audi raced down the dirt track leading away from the homestead towards the metal security gate. Even from a distance, they could see the control panel had been blasted with a gun and the gate was lying open.

"Slow down," Adam said they hurtled through the gate and on to the dirt track.

"Don't worry," she said looking in her rear mirror. The Mercedes Benz was following in hot pursuit.

At the junction with the A82, Izzy slowed the Audi down just enough to make sure they could get out on to the road safely. Now facing north, she put her foot down and raced along the main road running along Loch Lomond. As she expected, the road was busy with cars, buses and trucks all heading towards the upper Highlands.

"Can you see them?" she said to Adam. "Are they still behind us? How close are they?"

Adam craned his neck to look out the back window. In the distance, the Mercedes had got on to the A82 and was gunning towards them. The car swerved around slower moving vehicles, causing other road users to beep their horns as they cut in front of them.

"They're coming!" he said.

"That's what we want," she replied with glee.

Racing cars was one of the things Izzy loved doing and she was good at it. She'd been driving, albeit illegally, since the age of 12, and there was nothing she loved more than to speed along a dual carriageway, as the road was at that point. "We need them to keep following us. I've got an idea that may put them off our trail permanently."

Ten minutes later, they had reached Tarbet, a small hamlet by the west side of the loch which was little more than a hotel and a handful of buildings. Instead of going on to the A83 that would take them in the direction of Oban, at the junction with the Tarbet Hotel, Izzy turned right. It was still the A82, but gone was the dual carriageway. Instead, it was the narrow and winding original loch-side road.

"Where are we going?" Adam shouted as they sped past the hotel and onwards.

"North."

"And we're taking this road?"

Izzy didn't answer, merely smiled. She knew this road like the back of her hand and exactly how she was going to shake off the Mercedes and the evil bastards it was carrying. She just needed a particularly nasty bend in the road and something big like a tourist bus coming the opposite way.

"Are they still following?"

"Yes, and they're gaining on us." Adam's voice broke as he gripped the seat.

"Hold on to your hat!" she quipped.

The car sped up again, and Izzy yelled in delight as she took it around some hairy corners, corners that on one side were the steep sides of the mountains and on the other, a crash barrier and the deep dark depths of Loch Lomond.

"Wooohooo!" she shouted as they took another one. She glanced at Adam who looked like he was doing his best not to be sick.

"You okay?"

"No, but there's not much I can do about it." he said, face a little green.

"Have they sped up?" She looked in her rear mirror. The Mercedes was gaining on them. She could almost make out the features of the driver and the passenger in the front.

Adam peered over his shoulder, gulping. "Yes."

"Great." Izzy gleefully bounced in her seat. "Not much longer."

They reached a point in the road that Adam knew was close to the top of the road, a place where many a poor traveller had met their end. It was on a blind bend, almost a hairpin turn, and he closed his eyes unable to watch the craziness that was about to unfold. Although a very experienced driver, and even though the Mercedes Benz was gaining on them fast, Izzy slowed down as she drove the car around it. The Audi hugged the bend and squeaked around the corner just as the Inverness to Glasgow Stagecoach bus was approaching from the other side. Izzy smiled as they whizzed past it.

You beauty! She put her foot down on the accelerator pedal. As the Audi roared away, all they could hear was the prolonged sound of the bus horn, the screeching of brakes and a bang as something hit something metallic at speed. Splash! A vehicle was in the loch and Izzy knew it wasn't the bus, for in her mirror, she could see it was still on the road.

"Bingo!" she shouted as she slowed the car down and looked for a turning spot.

"What? What happened?" Adam asked as he tried to see.

"I think we've just rid ourselves of some very nasty men," she said with a smile.

Izzy did a three-point turn and drove the car back the way they had come. Neither of them said anything as she pulled up behind the bus and got out. She walked around the bus to see the bus driver and a couple of passengers standing looking at a car submerged some way out in the loch. The driver was on the phone reporting the accident.

"Can we help?" she asked one of the passengers, a man in his 30s.

"No, there's nothing you can do," he replied. "The car is too far out."

"Did you see what happened?"

"They came speeding around the corner on the wrong side and nearly hit the bus. If it hadn't been for the quick thinking of the driver putting on the brakes, they would have hit the bus. Instead, they swerved and hit the barrier. The car took off and landed over there. It was like a scene from a movie."

He pointed to a spot in the dark loch where the back of the Mercedes could be seen sticking up out of the water.

"Do you think there are any survivors?"

The man shrugged. "I'd go in to have a look, but the driver said the loch is too dangerous to swim in, especially at this time of year. The water's freezing and there's all sorts of nasty currents. He's called the emergency services, and they're sending a boat out from Balloch."

Izzy nodded and then motioned for Adam to follow her back to the car. They got in.

"Now what?" Adam asked.

"Now, we go home."

Chapter 21 - Home

After the accident, Izzy drove Adam back to the farmhouse and immediately rushed into the house to switch on her police scanner to check for news of the crash. Sure enough, the radio waves were full of information about the occupants of the Mercedes Benz. There were two dead at the scene, one identified as Michael Creedie, a well-known criminal from London, and another one was rushed to hospital with serious injuries. Izzy whooped when she heard the news.

"Fantastic!" she said grinning at Adam. "Aaron won't need to worry about them anymore."

"What about the one that survived?"

Izzy smiled. "He won't bother us again," she said. "There's a good chance he'll die, but if he survives and comes back, I'll put a bullet through his head."

"You're a scary woman," Adam joked.

"You don't know the half of it!" Izzy wound her arms around Adam's neck and gave him a lingering kiss. "Right, let's get them all back and celebrate."

They were a lively party that evening revelling in their success in not only saving the boys from slavery, but in ridding Aaron of his pimp for good. Mary made a huge lasagne which they ate with roast potatoes and salad. Izzy cracked open a couple of bottles of champagne and they toasted their good fortune. Even Aaron was allowed a half glass and was soon rosy-faced from the alcohol.

After everyone had finished eating, Izzy stood up and held up her glass. "I'd like to say a toast," she began. "I'd like to say thank you to the team for supporting me on this mission, to Aaron who was a fantastic researched and to Adam, without whom, none of those boys would have been saved."

"Hear hear!" Dinghy slapped the table.

Izzy sat down and Adam stood up.

"And I'd also like to raise a toast to Izzy who not only saved my life, but rescued Aaron and the boys. Without her, I wouldn't be here and for that I'll be forever grateful. To Izzy!"

"To Izzy!"

Adam sat down and then Aaron stood up with his glass.

"No more toasts!" Dinghy yelled. "I think we've had enough!"

"No, I'd really like say something." The boy seemed a little choked up. "Izzy I just wanted to say thank you for bringing me back to Scotland, for giving me a home and for rescuing me from Estelle. Everyone has been so nice here and, well, they've really made me feel welcome and you all feel like family and…" Tears welled in his eyes. He quickly wiped them. "To everyone!"

"To everyone!"

The party lasted until 11pm when the exhausted inhabitants of Crann Darach went up to bed for an untroubled sleep.

The following morning, after Adam discovered Izzy was not up for an early morning quickie due to there being other people in the house, he made a decision. It was about time he took his woman away for a real holiday. He thought about taking her abroad, but quickly ruled that out. No, it should be somewhere close, somewhere romantic and somewhere he could wine and dine her properly. He scrolled through websites on his mobile Looking for ideas of where to take her. Then a thought occurred to him, and he smiled. He knew the perfect place to take her.

"Iz," he said, as she returned from having a shower. Her hair was wrapped up in a hand towel, and she had on a fluffy white robe.

"Uh-huh?" She sat down at her dressing table and took her hair out of the towel. It flopped on to her shoulders, and she immediately took up a brush and began to take the tangles out.

"How do you fancy a few days away?"

"That sounds lovely," she replied, distracted by her hair.

"Starting today."

Izzy's brush stopped midair and she rotated to look at him. "Alright," she said. "But where will be go?"

"Just leave that to me," he replied. "I'll make it a surprise."

"But what do I need to bring with me? Are we going abroad or staying at home?"

"Home."

"Posh or normal?"

"Posh."

"Are you going to give me a clue as to where we are going?"

"I'll tell you when we get there," he said.

"You've already booked it, haven't you?"

Adam said nothing more and reclined back in bed with a satisfied smile.

****

The Gleneagles Hotel was opened by the Caledonian Railway in 1924 in Auchterarder near Perth. One of only a handful of hotels in Scotland to boast of a uber-luxury AA Red Five Star rating, the Georgian style hotel was also home to many international golf tournaments. But golf was the last thing on his mind when Adam booked a few days there for him and Izzy.

They arrived later that afternoon and Izzy gasped when she saw their room. It was beautifully decorated in an opulent style and had a massive four-poster bed. She dropped her bags and threw herself onto the plush sheets.

"This is amazing," she said. "I can't believe you brought me here. I've always wanted to come here."

Adam laughed and shut the room door. "Only the best for you," he said. He threw the key card on a table, slipped off his shoes and joined her on the bed. They lay there together for a few moments before Adam spoke again.

"Izzy, I have something I need to say." Izzy lifted her head from where it was resting on his chest. "Well, it's something I need to ask."

"Okay, go ahead, ask me anything." She kissed him lightly on the lips.

"Well," he began, "it's just that the last week or so you seem to have no problem with…killing people…"

Izzy waited for the punchline. Was this going to be a deal breaker for their relationship?

"…and I just wondered if you could explain…why." His facial expression gave nothing away of his inner thoughts.

Izzy bit her lip, sighing. "Okay, well, promise me you won't freak out?"

"I promise. I know you well enough to know you're not some psycho." He smiled reassuringly.

"Okay, well…how shall I put this?" She racked her brains. How did you tell someone you're in love with that you kill people for money? "I'm sort of a killer for hire…an assassin…"

Izzy waited for his reaction. What she wasn't expecting was for him to burst out laughing.

"No, I mean, really…what do you really do for a living?"

"I really am an assassin." She stared at him without any hint of humour. "I kill people for money. But it's bad people. I don't kill good people."

Adam pulled away slightly, his eyes roaming over her face for a few moments. Her stomach clenched in fear. This will be the part where he tells me goodbye, she thought. It seemed like an age before he spoke again.

"Okay," he said. "I can live with that."

She let out a sigh of relief.

"And it's only bad people you kill?" Adam wrapped his arms around her, cuddling her close.

"Yes."

He kissed her on the lips, then stopped. "So, how much does someone make being an assassin?"

Izzy smiled. "A shitload of money."

"Uh. I'd always wondered," he said. "And…roughly…how much would that be in a year?"

"Adam Harrison," Izzy said with faux exasperation, "are you going to ask me questions all afternoon, or are we going to get down and dirty?"

"My mind has suddenly gone blank," he joked, and he went in for another kiss.

And now I'm delighted to bring you the first chapter in the next book in the series...Wrath.

Wrath

T WELLS BROWN

Chapter 1

"Mother. Mother. Mother." Vanity might be my girl but she was a serious pain in my ass.

"Do not fucking call me that." These girls were going to be the death of me. "Don't call me Mother, Mommy, Mami, Mom, not even Mommy Dearest. Any of those come out of any of your mouths and I'll visit you in the middle of the night… you'll know I was there by the mess I leave behind."

Vanity a.k.a. Catalina snickered. She always had a wicked sense of humor. I was the closest to her of all the sisters, I hope this didn't change things between us but I knew this like I knew the color of my skin I could count on her. I could count on all the girls to some degree, but some of them you just had to count on messing up. Or going off the rails. Never Vanity, she mostly did what she was supposed to as long as it didn't mess up her nails. I understood this about her, so it made it easy for me to keep her close at a time like this.

"Well, what is going to be your title? You just gonna go about acting like nothing has changed? You're in charge of all of us now. You're also in charge of dealing with Conexus and helping the board rebuild. How awesome would it be if there was actually somebody who looked like us there? You know, somebody with a uterus."

"I have no idea what my new code name is. I'm Wrath, I like it, I embrace it, it's me."

"Yes, but you're so much more now. You're in charge of the assignments. You're in control of who gets to come into SOS... and who gets to stay. You're in charge of dealing with the Conexus board and keeping them in line. You are so much more than just Wrath, you're gonna need to embrace it. Step up, girl. What're you waiting for?"

I wasn't really sure what was going on and hadn't settled into my role. Mother, the past mother who was really fucking good at what she did left me in charge. I have no idea why or what made her think I would be the ideal person to manage all of these bitches. But here I was stepping into a role I had zero interest in. I knew what I had to do. Evil was at play, and if there was one thing I couldn't abide by, that was evil. It's the reason I went into this, fighting for my life on the streets of New York in little Puerto Rico taught me well and truly how to take care of me. Joining the Sisters of Sin was what brought the world back to me. If not for the original Mother, I'd have lost my life at the ripe old age of 23. How was I ever going to be her?

How was I ever going to live up to the example she set? The bar was indeed high, but for some reason, she thought I could do it, everyone thought I could do it, even the girls. The only one who had a problem with me being Mother was the leader of the Conexus board, Jeff Lindsay.

But Jeff was a traditionalist; he believed the way things have been done, is how things should continue to be done. Therefore, even though he was against me becoming Mother, he honored her right to name her own successor. Through gritted teeth, the ceremony went through. None of the girls were allowed to be there. None of us knew what mother had to go through to become all that she was, how the men forced an incoming mother to stand bare naked before them, and fight for her life to prove she could... or she died.

I fought four men. Four clothed, armed men, with my bare hands, naked as the day I was born. One champion for each board member. I defeated them because my superpower was my ability to hold down on one single thing and make it happen. So, the first one came at me with a baseball bat which I removed from his possession immediately and bashed his head in.

The second one came at me with a knife. He would be a little trickier because he knew my first order would be to take his weapon, so instead, I jumped on his shoulders and stuck my thumbs in his eyes. He dropped the knife immediately and tried to pull me off of him.

I wasn't going anywhere.

As soon as we hit the ground I rolled, grabbed the knife, and cut his throat.

Number three was a little smarter, he didn't bring a weapon to the fight. He was a big fucker, with a thick neck, and a bald head, but he had one fatal flaw... He had a face full of hair. In fact, his entire body was covered in hair, too bad I didn't have any fire. I watched him not sure what the big meathead was going to do first. He watched me knowing I had just taken out the two that had come before him. That was my advantage, he was wary of me. I relaxed and covered my breasts and my groin.

In my most feminine voice, "I've at least earned a shirt to cover myself, haven't I?"

His eyes brightened slightly.

"Come on, give me your shirt." I shivered and curled my shoulders in.

He watched me with suspicious eyes. Wow, I couldn't blame him. I swayed my shoulders back-and-forth and tilted my head and looked him straight in the eye.

"I took out the first two, I deserve to be covered. I've earned it, you know I have." I lowered my chin to my chest and took my eyes off him. That's when he rushed me but he was so sure of himself that he didn't pay attention as I dropped to a crouch grabbed his ankles and flipped him back over me. The fool landed on his meathead and knocked himself out. I stood over his body and waited for him to wake up. I could see his chest rise and fall but he didn't move. I stepped back.

The same raspy voice came over the loudspeaker that had been directing this bloodbath.

"Step back against the wall." I did as I was instructed and took that moment to position myself to see out the door when it opened. I wanted to make sure I saw every single face of every single man in this place. I made eye contact with another mammoth of a man who entered with, I shit you not, a mace. I pushed off the wall with excitement. This was my first weapon of choice when I was getting started. I had many versions of it over the years, my first being crude and homemade, until now where my collection was vast and historic.

I love weapons. Weapons of all kinds. I didn't care. My goal was to use every weapon ever made and make a couple of my own. I didn't discriminate, which meant I knew a little bit about everything… but I digress.

This weapon I knew. As he approached his steps faltered. I

couldn't help but smile. I mean I probably smiled a little too big and showed a little too much of my pearly whites, but I couldn't believe it. It was almost as if one of them didn't do their homework. We were supposed to be the biggest and the most effective spy and assassin network in the world and they didn't know about my mace collection? Or was somebody giving me a little bit of help?

I had a feeling wash over me and I swore I smelled gardenias. The scent has me smiling again. She was with me, Mother. I was going to be okay. Not that I'd doubted, it but this made me secure in the knowledge of it.

I'm not gonna go into the gory details but let's just say the man ended up with a mace in the top of his head. I was careful not to get any blood on the shirt because I wanted to cover up as soon as I had him down. I had him stripped of his shirt in three seconds flat and I wanted out of that fucking place.

No wonder Mother was such a bitch most of the time. No wonder she was so strict with us after everything she'd gone through just to become Mother.

Holy Crap!

If anybody knew this was how you reached a leadership role with the Conexus, at least a sa woman, the position would go away. And here I am unable to warn the next mother of what she would have to endure. It didn't sit very well with me. I didn't like the idea of staying part of this patriarchal bull shit being run by entitled old men.

Of course the lazy men could not be bothered to fight me

on their own. No. Not that way. They would not win against me. They knew it and I knew it.

They were hoping that their champions would defeat me. Then what?

I looked into what and why I was being forced to do this. Turns out t was nothing more than Jeff Lyndsay being what he referredto as a traditionalist who went by the letter of the law. Because I was not yet Mother I could not name a successor and if their champions were to strike me down the Coexus would then be able to name a successor instead other than a Sister. It was a loophole set in place to keep the Sisters of Sin running smoothly. It was a loophole Jeff Lindsay was working hard to exploit.

The man would rather have seen me dead than allow me to assume the role of Mother. It was too much power for someone he couldn't control. I wondered what Mother had done to keep him in line.

Showing his true colors to me was a major flaw of his, and an epic mistake. I loved nothing more than to learn people's weaknesses and how do you learn their weaknesses, by paying attention to their strengths. His arrogance and his unwavering adherence to the letter of the law. Of course, it was subjective. There was one rule for the Conexus board, a whole separate set of rules for the Sisters of Sin. And yet another set of rules for normal people. The man valued power over all.

I did defeat the champions, obviously, 'cause I'm still here taking on a role I never thought I would have or wanted. I didn't want it … but I took it, becuase I didn't know what else to do. The first thing I did was write a letter and submitted it to the" powers that be" as to who would be my successor. Then I did something even further and named three more Sisters in case those girls weren't around. Last thing I needed was for the Conexus to start knocking off my assassins. Therefore, I made a back up plan to my back up plan.

I did not trust this Conexus. The board was fractured at best, contaminated with self righteous men who believed their words meant law. I was over it but knew better than to buck the system to their faces or I'd never survive the first hurdle.

I was a girl who thrived on back up plans, alternative versions of everything. The one thing a gal could count on was that shit would go sideways. Therefore, I sent each of the girls a letter not to be opened unless I died naming my successors in order of priority.

Jeff Lindsay was doing everything in his power to put it back together the way that it was before. That was something else we were going to address. It was time to make some changes and bring the Conexus into the new century. An all white, all male board that ruled an all female multi racial assassin organization was not going to work anymore.

A few of the sisters had already begun questioning some of our assignments.

Something about Jeff had always set my teeth on edge. I didn't like any of the board members but I didn't like very many people in general so I wasn't a very good judge of character.

I liked working on my own. I also enjoyed jumping in and helping some of the other girls when they needed me. But mostly, I was a solo artist. How was I supposed to get used to working with everybody… all the time? My desire to kill had not diminished, so taking over Mother's duties meant I was going to have to streamline my own work. Because the desire to kill the bad guys was never going away. It was the only thing that allowed me the few precious hours of sleep at night. And if I didn't do something to appease the wrath I felt anytime somebody got away with hurting an innocent, that bitch would emerge and leave scorched earth in her wake.

"Will you have to spend much time in Rome?" I knew what Vanity was doing. She was trying to see how much of my workload she could take. I'd like to believe it was to be helpful, but, this girl liked her money. And she had an incredible partner, Juan Carlos who liked her. He did whatever he could to assist her on assignment, which was walking the line, but unless I wanted to lose her I had to let her do her thing. The two had started working with Juan Carlos' security firm since he'd gone private, leaving Spain's version of the secret service. I suspected he still did favors… but favors were how the game was played in our world.

"I'll be heading to Rome in a few days. I want to keep an eye on the board members they recruit." Like I said; I didnt trust the men at the top.

"What about Dominika?"

"She's mine."

"Yes, I understand and honesty, if you hadn't become Mother I wouldn't even care, but since you are Mother and she offed our last one, I'd like in on the hunt. If nothing more than to make sure it's done correctly."

"What are you proposing?"

"I'm proposing that you allow Juan Carlos to use his magical skills to find out where Dominika is. And that you allow me and my mighty fine man to secure her for you."

"I'll accept this help on one condition. Nobody kills her but me." It was my right as the new leader of our girl gang to take out the one who had gone against us. She'd been undermining the sisterhood for much longer than any of us realized and we weren't on solid footing anymore.

Assassins were typically good at adjusting. But we were not normal assassins. We right the wrongs. How were we supposed to right the wrongs when everything was wrong?

Discerning what was right was becoming harder and harder.

How could we trust the assignments we went to carry out were for justice and not power? Their power. The men who made the decisions on who would live and who would die.

These were important questions I needed answers for. Our sisterhood used to have faith in the Conexus board... but we'd lost that.

Were we still working for justice and not power? I needed to know. It was crucial the sisterhood have faith in the Conexus board. We'd lost faith after everything we'd found out about Dominika and her influence with Jeff Lindsey. It came as a great shock that she'd had an affair with him early on. And then killing our one and only Mother? I don't care who you are, I don't care how badass you think you are, you come after one of my girls? I'm gonna take your ass out.

No question, no problem, you'll be dead. And my girls needed to know that. They needed to know that even if the board that governed them would not watch out and stick up for them, I would.

I wasn't gonna let them down. I wasn't gonna let Mother down. For some crazy ass reason she thought I could handle this. She'd always seen more in me than I had. For a long time I lived her version of me and not mine. Before long I became her version of me, instead of the version I was. Her version was better. In her version, I lived and thrived. In my version, I was going to make it six months past meeting her. I was in a deep spiral and all I wanted was somebody to take me out of this world.

Today? I'm good with myself. I remove people from this world who hurt others. And I'm not talking about a little hurt, I'm talking about men who are essentially mass murderers and slave traders. Men who destroy communities, cities, towns... countries. That is the evil I go after and I'm here to tell you I enjoy every single moment of it. Every kill is a reward and a badge I wear proudly.

Other Books in the Series

Vanity	ISBN: 978-1-73333 07-6-3
Greed	ISBN: 978-1-9163520-6-3
Pride	ISBN: 978-1-922448-43-9
Jealousy	ISBN: 978-1-7360951-1-9
Lust	ISBN: 979820120351
Envy	ISBN: 978-1-9163520-7-0
Wrath	(available December 5)
Passion	ISBN: 979884742999 (available January 5)
Dominika	ASIN B0B9HWK3XB

About the Author

Dawn (D A) Nelson is an award-winning Scottish author of books for both children and adults. She writes action-packed romantic thrillers and dark comedies for adults as well as fantasy adventures for kids. Apart from writing for the SOS series, Dawn is also planning a fantasy/steampunk series for adults too. Her first book was a kids' novel, DarkIsle, which won the Royal Mail Scottish Children's Book Awards (8-12 age group) in 2007.

Dawn lives in a small country village on the banks of the River Clyde, just a stone's throw away from the beautiful Loch Lomond. She lives there with her two kids, three small dogs and three chickens. In her spare time, Dawn loves to read and enjoys both literary, romance and fantasy books. When not writing or reading, Dawn loves to bake and watch movies.

https://danelsonauthor.com/

Social Media

Facebook: https://www.facebook.com/authordanelson
Twitter: https://twitter.com/danelsonauthor
LinkedIn: https://www.linkedin.com/in/dawn-nelson-95210221/
Tik Tok: https://www.tiktok.com/@danelson70

Pinterest: https://www.pinterest.co.uk/danelsonauthor/
Goodreads: https://www.goodreads.com/author/
show/1351494.D_A_Nelson

Dawn's Other Books

Greed

Berlin. Present Day.

It's a fact of life that opposites attract.
So, when SOS assassin Alex Greir, aka
Greed, bumps into Nick Walker in a
Berlin nightclub, sparks begin to fly.
An MI6 agent, Nick's been sent by the
British Government to infiltrate the
Sisters.

But, one look at the beautiful Alex and he's smitten.
He's got a new mission now: to tame the feisty blonde and make
her his own.

However, the gorgeous Alex has
other ideas. She's no pushover for a
handsome face.
Then she finds out who he really is...
And all hell breaks loose.
Gripping, sexy and electrifying, this is
the story of Greed.

Amazon: https://geni.us/cI4I
All other ebook retailers: https://books2read.com/u/bz159q

BOOKS FOR ADULTS

Dusting Down Alcudia

Nina Esposito, archaeologist, is on a mission. She's flying to Mallorca to locate a magnificent Roman treasure that's been lost for centuries.

But, when a former love and a work rival vie for her attention, Nina finds herself locked in romantic rollercoaster. Which one is truly worthy of her? And do they have ulterior motives other than winning her heart?

Added to the mix is a Spanish billionaire who will stop at nothing to get the jewels for himself.

Who will get to the treasure first? Will Nina's heart be broken along the way? And can she really trust either of the men in her life?

Join Nina on a breath-taking journey of discovery that takes her from the dusty fields of Mallorca to the diamond brokers of Amsterdam. As she soon finds out: there's everything to play for when you're Dusting Down Alcudia.

https://geni.us/alcudia

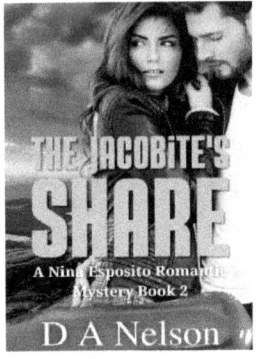

The Jacobite's Share

When an argument leads to estrangement from lover Jay, Nina decides to take a research job at a Scottish castle to get away from her troubles.

Back in her native land, the plucky archaeologist soon finds herself up to her ears in a centuries-old mystery and attempted murder.

Now she's got to find the Jacobite treasure before a would-be assassin picks off the handsome Laird and his equally gorgeous brother... a brother who has taken quite a shine to her.

And when Jay returns to her life, things will only get further complicated as his ex-fiancée shows up to create mayhem.

The second in the popular Nina Esposito Adventures, The Jacobite's Share is a fast-paced adventure thriller full of darkness and danger.

https://geni.us/jacobitesshare

Everything She Wants

When married Susan decides to run away with a Wham! tribute band as their 'Shirley', little does she know of the consequences it will bring. Fed up with her cold husband, desperate to get away from their spoiled teen daughter, she joins the group to find some happiness in her life. And she gets it - for a while. As the group gets more successful, Susan

finds herself
falling for an 80s pop heartthrob. Has
she finally found true love and will she
get everything she wants?

https://geni.us/everythingshewantsbook

BOOKS FOR KIDS (8-12 years)

THE DARKISLE TRILOGY

DarkIsle

For 10-year-old Morag, there's nothing magical about the cellar of her
cruel foster parents' home. But that's
where she meets Aldiss, a talking rat
and his resourceful companion, Bertie
the dodo. She jumps at the chance to
run away and join them on their race
against time to save their homeland
from an evil warlock named Devilish, who is intent on destroying it. But first Bertie and Aldiss will need to stop bickering long
enough to free the only guide who knows where to find Devilish: Shona, a dragon who's been turned
to stone. Terrifying, touching and funny,
DarkIsle is a vivid and fast-paced novel
of captivating originality.

https://geni.us/darkislenovel

DarkIsle: Resurrection (The Witch's Revenge)

The 2nd book in the DarkIsle trilogy. Two months after she saved The Eye of Lornish, Morag is adjusting to life in the secret northern kingdom of Marnoch Mor. But dark dreams are troubling her and a spate of unexplained events prove that even with the protection of her friends—Shona the dragon, Bertie the dodo and Aldiss the rat— Morag is still not safe from harm... The 1st book (DarkIsle) WON the 2008 Scottish Children's Book Awards.

https://geni.us/darkisleseries-book2

DarkIsle: The Final Battle

All seem well in Marnoch Mor. Bertie the dodo, Aldiss the rat and Shona the dragon are looking forward to a relaxing Christmas. However, Morag is having bad dreams – an old enemy is trying to reach her. And when another former foe turns up on her doorstep it is clear something is badly wrong.

Morag and her friends are soon forced to face a powerful new threat, one more terrifying than they have ever encountered before.

The battle for the DarkIsle of Murst must be won…or Marnoch Mor itself will be lost.

https://geni.us/darkisleseriesbook3

A Children's History of Glasgow

Have you ever wondered what it would have been like living in Glasgow when William Wallace was there? What about being a sailor on one of the ships owned by the rich tobacco lords in Georgian times? This book will uncover the important and exciting things that happened in your town. With a helpful timeline, fun imaginary accounts, cool old photos of places you ll recognize in Glasgow and amazing top facts and information, you will discover things in Children s History of Glasgow you never knew about your town. Investigate the people and events that have defined your home town: Who was St Mungo? Where was James Watt when he first thought of inventing the steam engine?

https://geni.us/historybookglasgow

www.ingramcontent.com/pod-product-compliance
Lightning Source LLC
Chambersburg PA
CBHW070008260626
47159CB00005B/1721